SUSAN NAPIER

Phantom Lover

Harlequin Books

TORONTO • NEW YORK • LONDON
AMSTERDAM • PARIS • SYDNEY • HAMBURG
STOCKHOLM • ATHENS • TOKYO • MILAN
MADRID • WARSAW • BUDAPEST • AUCKLAND

If you purchased this book without a cover you should be aware
that this book is stolen property. It was reported as "unsold and
destroyed" to the publisher, and neither the author nor the
publisher has received any payment for this "stripped book."

ISBN 0-373-11707-8

PHANTOM LOVER

Copyright © 1994 by Susan Napier.

All rights reserved. Except for use in any review, the reproduction or
utilization of this work in whole or in part in any form by any electronic,
mechanical or other means, now known or hereafter invented, including
xerography, photocopying and recording, or in any information storage
or retrieval system, is forbidden without the written permission of the
publisher, Harlequin Enterprises Limited, 225 Duncan Mill Road,
Don Mills, Ontario, Canada M3B 3K9.

All characters in this book have no existence outside the imagination of
the author and have no relation whatsoever to anyone bearing the same
name or names. They are not even distantly inspired by any individual
known or unknown to the author, and all incidents are pure invention.

This edition published by arrangement with Harlequin Enterprises B.V.

® and TM are trademarks of the publisher. Trademarks indicated with
® are registered in the United States Patent and Trademark Office, the
Canadian Trade Marks Office and in other countries.

Printed in U.S.A.

CHAPTER ONE

'WELL, am I under arrest?'

Honor stared across the battered wooden table at the irritatingly fresh-faced female police constable. Old age must really be creeping up on her if policemen and women had started to look like schoolchildren. Suddenly she felt every one of her creaking twenty-five years!

'Not yet. Right now you're simply helping us with our enquiries,' the constable said, with a complacency Honor found equally irritating.

'So this is entirely voluntary, right? If I want to I can walk out of here without answering any of your questions,' she said, to emphasise that she wasn't prepared to be pushed around any longer.

Her wits were starting to return at last and she bitterly regretted having allowed herself to be bundled into the police car in the first place. But she had been so confused, so utterly mortified that she hadn't cared how she retreated from the scene of her embarrassment, as long as it was at high speed! The police had been extremely efficient in that respect at least, but now they were being stupidly stubborn about letting her go.

'You *could* do that,' said the older, non-uniformed man leaning against the wall on the opposite side of the tiny interview-room. 'But that would mean that we would have to make a decision as to whether to let you go or charge you. And I can tell you that on the evidence so far I would have to come down on the side of an immediate arrest. In that case you'd be held in custody until tomorrow's court sitting. Your lawyer could then apply for bail but we would naturally oppose and you could well find yourself a guest of the government until your trial. Given the backlog in the Auckland Courts, that could be months...'

Honor blanched. With the currently uneven state of her finances the idea of involving lawyers was far more of a disincentive than summary incarceration. At least one didn't have to *pay* to be in prison!

She had forgotten the plain-clothes man's name but he had introduced himself as a detective inspector from Auckland Central and she supposed that she should be grateful that he had hauled her off to a nearby police station rather than taken her straight back to the city. If only Harry, the local constable, had been involved she might have been able to laugh it all off, but this was evidently a city-based operation that had spilled out into the rural fringes of Auckland, and explaining herself to strangers was a great deal more difficult.

She sighed, and glumly eyed the senior officer. At least he looked on the wrong side of thirty, with enough experience of human life to have a bit of sympathy for people caught up in awkward situations of none of their own making...well, almost none.

He was watching her now, with shrewd eyes that were neither overtly accusing nor condemning, merely shrewdly assessive. Not at all like the glassy-eyed suspicion that was being directed at her by the ambitious WPC.

'Now, Miss Sheldon, why don't you tell us why you were skulking about Mr Blake's house?'

Trust that young whippersnapper to choose the most offensive way to put her question. Or should that be whippersnapperette? Good grief, now she was even *thinking* like an old woman!

'I wasn't skulking,' Honor told her firmly. 'I have never skulked in my entire life.'

'Then what were you doing lurking on his property?'

'I was *not* lurking——'

'I think we've established that Miss Sheldon was on the property, Gibbons,' the DI interrupted, and for a moment Honor could have sworn she saw a glimmer of humour in the cold grey eyes.

Gibbons. What a good name for her, Honor thought with malicious satisfaction, squinting to deliberately obscure the other woman's attractive features. Yes, with her shaggy, reddish-brown hair and long arms she might just pass for a female gibbon in the murk of the jungle. Or was that orang-utan? Or baboon? All three summoned suitably derogatory images that boosted Honor's bruised confidence. Being somewhat short and generously rounded, stricken with freckles and thick wavy hair of nondescript brown that refused to obey any cut or style, no matter how professional, Honor had long ago given up worrying needlessly about her appearance, but under that supercilious uniformed stare she was beginning to feel like a total degenerate. In fact, she could feel definite latent criminal tendencies beginning to surface. A desire to indulge in a little police baiting...

'Miss Sheldon?'

'What?' As usual in moments of crisis, Honor's thoughts had wandered disastrously from the point.

'Now we need to establish exactly why you were visiting the Blake residence in such a... shall we say, unconventional fashion?' This time the grey eyes were definitely affable—suspiciously so.

'I don't see what's unconventional about a bicycle,' Honor countered defensively, suddenly wondering if she was victim of a good-cop, bad-cop interrogation technique that was supposed to lull her into a false sense of security.

'You hid it in some bushes,' the young baboon pointed out as if it countenanced a crime in itself.

Honor frowned. She wasn't going to tell this snotty kid that she had been ashamed of her battered bike of dubious vintage and even more dubious brake-power.

When she had set out from home she had been expecting her destination to be the usual friendly homestead common to most New Zealand rural properties, albeit an up-market one commensurate with the size and diversity of Blake Investments. Instead she had been presented with a view of an intimidatingly pretentious mansion at the bottom of a steeply sloping, thickly gravelled driveway that sent cold chills up her spine. She had had nightmare visions of herself not being able to stop, ploughing straight on through the majestic front door, muddy tyres mowing down the butler and scattering screaming maids in all directions. Oh, yes, that would make a grand first—and last—impression on the man she had come to see!

'I didn't want it to get stolen,' she temporised on a half-truth, unable to resist adding, 'Of course, I didn't know at the time that there were hordes of police already *lurking* and *skulking* around the property.'

The constable reddened, while the DI coughed, his hand briefly covering his mouth. Having abandoned his laid-back lean on the wall, he sat down on the other spare chair and put his big hands flat on the table.

'Let's cut all the clever word-play and get down to brass tacks, shall we? All we want to know, Miss Sheldon, is why you were visiting Mr Blake on this particular day, claiming an acquaintance that he himself emphatically denies. And why you previously tried to threaten him over the telephone. It was you, wasn't it, trying to contact him on the telephone at eight thirty-five a.m. this morning? You have a clear and beautifully distinctive voice that is very easily identifiable.'

Honor bristled, ignoring the compliment. Was that what this fuss was all about—her abortive phone call? 'I didn't try to threaten him. Is that what they said? I wasn't even allowed to *speak* to him!'

'I know. You spoke to me.' His cool admission scotched *that* particular theory. If he had been already there to pick up the phone then it wasn't her call that had prompted police action.

'Has somebody been kidnapped?' she asked, all sorts of awful possibilities suddenly occurring to her.

Her question was quietly ignored. 'You refused to tell me what your call was about, except that you had written Adam Blake some letters and that you wanted to talk to him about them.'

'It was personal,' she said stubbornly, feeling herself begin to blush as she remembered the rather garbled conversation she had engaged in before quickly hanging up, obviously thwarting the trace on the call that the stonewalling she had received had been designed to permit.

She had hoped to be able to avoid the risk of humiliation in person but, her phone call having failed so miserably, she had been left with no honourable choice but to cycle the fifteen kilometres from her home at Kowhai Hill to the address of the Blake homestead. If her car hadn't been held hostage for the past week by the local mechanic who was waiting for a vital spare part she might have driven and thereby perhaps avoiding any necessity to *skulk*.

'So you've already said. But I think that your very presence here establishes the fact that whatever it is is no longer a purely personal matter,' it was pointed out with inescapable logic.

'I don't see why I should be treated like a criminal just because I went visiting uninvited,' Honor said sullenly. They would probably laugh themselves sick when she told them. Either that or charge her with wasting valuable police time.

'Extortion *is* a crime,' the constable intoned sternly.

'Extortion!' Honor's beautifully distinctive voice creaked like an old rusty gate, her green eyes widening in horror.

'Extortion,' confirmed the DI heavily. 'Or blackmail, if you want to put it in its more common emotive term.'

Blackmail?

Oh, *hell*!

Suddenly what had been merely an embarrassing misunderstanding took on hideously serious complications.

Honor's truculent resistance crumbled. She squeezed her eyes tight shut to combat the sinking realisation that she really wasn't going to escape without giving a very thorough account of her actions to the police.

And all because of that damned Shakespearean sonnet she had mooned over this morning!

CHAPTER TWO

DARLING,
Is it thy will thy image should keep open
My heavy eyelids to the weary night?
Dost thou desire my slumbers should be broken,
While shadows, like to thee, do mock my sight?

The idea that her ordinary self could engender such wild longings in a man that he couldn't sleep at night was so bizarre that Honor's green eyes glowed with amused delight.

She picked up the cup of tea that she had just brewed for herself when she had heard the postman's whistle, and carried her precious letter over to the comfortable chair behind the untidy desk that served to designate part of the lounge of her small cottage as an office. She settled down in her familiar sprawl, a jean-clad leg slung over one padded chair arm, and scanned the rest of the Shakespearean sonnet, down to the last, jealous couplet:

For thee watch I, whilst thou dost wake elsewhere,
From me far off, with others all-too-near.

She couldn't help smiling. Others? There were certainly no 'others' in the sense that the sonnet suggested. The small community of Kowhai Hill, tucked in below the Waitakare Ranges just north-west of Auckland, wasn't exactly bulging with eligible males, and those she did come into contact with generally knew her too well to suffer any sleeplessness on her account. For one thing she was distressingly plain. For another, her reputation was as spotless as her name.

'Good old Honor' was a mate, someone with whom a local lad could be seen having a drink at the pub

11

without being accused of unfaithfulness by his girlfriend or wife, a woman whose social life consisted largely of group outings or happily 'making up the numbers' at dinner parties where she could be relied upon to fit in, regardless of the age or diversity of the company.

Except to Adam. To Adam she was someone quite different: a woman enticing in her mystery, challenging in her intellect, desirable in her elusiveness.

Honor's smile had disappeared by the time she reached the bottom of the page, its place taken by a vivid blush. Adam's prose might not have the unique beauty of Shakespeare's poetry, but it was none the less powerful stuff, a passionate outburst of feeling that was lyrical in its erotic intensity.

Although she had never met him in person, in eight months of correspondence Honor had formed a mental picture of a warm, witty and literate man whose love of writing cloaked a personal shyness that made him quite content to pursue their acquaintance entirely through correspondence.

Their letters had been a lively exchange of ideas about books, places, philosophies and world events rather than mundane personal details. Although she had learned that he was thirty-five, owned his own development company and lived on Auckland's North Shore, that was about the extent of her knowledge of his physical existence outside his letters.

But with the last six letters, her cosy conclusions about him had been exploded. Not only had they arrived weekly instead of at the usual monthly intervals, they were so joltingly different in emotional tenor that Honor would have thought they were penned by someone else if she hadn't recognised Adam's distinctive handwriting.

At first Honor had not known how to reply. What *did* you say to a man who suddenly told you that you were the only thing that gave his life hope and meaning and that your letters were his lifeline? When he begged you to believe that he had fallen wildly in love for the

first time in his life? That although he had never had
you, except in his illicit imagination, he missed you savagely in his heart, his arms, his bed...?

She had been amused. And enchanted. Apprehensive
and intrigued. And...yes, in spite of herself, *seduced*...

So, after the second letter, she had gathered her own
courage and replied according to the dictates of her
wayward heart rather than her sceptical head. Amazingly
the words had flowed out of her pen as if they had been
in there all along, awaiting the perfect moment to escape
the repression of her earnest common sense. No one ever
fell in love through the post, for goodness' sake! She
didn't even know what he *looked* like!

'All my love, Adam'.

She sighed as she reached the end of the second, sizzling page. Unlike his other letters, which often ran to
nine or ten pages, these passionate outpourings were invariably as short as they were hot and sweet.

She began to fold the delicate, onion-skin sheets along
the sharp crease-lines only to discover that there was a
third sheet, stuck to the second by some of the ink which
had run along the edges.

Carefully she peeled it free and froze as a name leapt
out at her from the few hastily scrawled lines.

I know we're not supposed to meet but if I don't
get to see your beautiful face soon, my darling, cour-
ageous Helen...touch the soft spun gold of your
hair...make love to your lush mouth and delicate body
the way I've dreamed of these last months I'll go mad!
Please come to me... Don't put me through the agony
of having to wait any longer. I need you...

Helen?
Helen!
Honor bolted upright in her chair.
Beautiful face?
Spun gold hair!

She swivelled her head to stare at her reflection in the blank grey computer screen which sat on her desk. By no stretch of the imagination could the unruly brown curls that tumbled around her shoulders be described as spun gold. Or the oval face sprinkled with freckles and rendered stern by the thick straight brows be considered beautiful. Her nose, rather pink from the spring cold that she was just shaking off, was the only thing about her that was glowing. And no one in his or her right mind would call her sturdy figure 'delicate'...

Her confusion turned to dawning horror.

Frantically she tugged open the stubborn bottom drawer of her desk and sorted through the sheaf of letters, carefully filed by date. Most of the envelopes were typed, addressed to Miss H. Sheldon at Rural Delivery, Kowhai Hill.

Her hands shaking, Honor opened some at random, scanning the opening lines.

The later, passionate letters were headed 'Darling', the rest were teasing salutes to 'M'Lady', a reference to the whimsical valentine card addressed to 'My Lady of the Moonlight' that had arrived by special delivery the day after the St Valentine's Ball in nearby Evansdale, which Honor had helped organise for a children's charity. She had been one of the hostesses and had introduced and been introduced to so many new people that night that all their names and faces had intermingled in her hazy recollection. She couldn't remember an Adam at all but there was no doubt from the handwritten rhyme inside his card, referring to roses and moonlight and ladies in distress, that he had known exactly who she was.

After all she *had* been pretty distressed that night, desperately fighting off the summer flu that she had later succumbed to, wandering the small memorial gardens in the moonlight while the dancing went on inside the adjacent community hall, trying to rid herself of a murderous headache that had refused to respond to the pills she had swallowed.

She had finally dozed off on a cramped park bench, waking an hour or so later to find herself tucked under a light rug in the back seat of her car, a sheaf of deep red roses lying on the seat beside her—obviously illegally picked in the gardens. Since there had been any number of hefty farming friends at the ball who could have performed the kindly deed she hadn't thought twice about it until she had received the stranger's valentine the next day. Then she had been curious, and yielded to the temptation of the implicit and very untraditional invitation of a post-office box number on the flap of the envelope.

She pulled out more letters until she had gone through them all and then began stuffing them haphazardly back into their envelopes, trying to control her rising panic at the awful realisation:

Not once in all their correspondence had he actually addressed her as 'Honor'! And her own trademark signature—a large, dramatic H with the other letters of her name an illiterate scrawl that she had fondly imagined was dashingly sophisticated—that too could have easily been misread.

'Honor?'

Her head snapped up. A yawning figure appeared in the doorway, her delicate, willowy figure clothed in the merest excuse for a nightgown, her long blonde hair spilling in disarray across her slender shoulders.

Honor's heart sank into her practical shoes at the sight of her guest. She could hear fate laughing like a drain in her ear.

'You're up early, Helen. It's only eleven o'clock.'

Her sarcasm went completely over her beautiful sister's head. 'Is it? I'd better get a move on, then. My flight leaves at three and Trina is taking me to lunch at the Regent before she zips me out to the airport.'

Her sister got lunches with her New Zealand agent at the best hotel in town and a lift to the airport in a limo, Honor ate cheese sandwiches in her kitchen and drove

an ageing Volkswagen. And God forbid that she offer
to farewell her sister at the airport. Helen hated to feel
'emotionally pressured', dismissing Honor's ready sensitivity as 'mawkishness'. That about summed up the
differences in their lifestyles—and their personalities,
Honor thought ruefully.

Honor had spent her teenage years watching with a
mixture of awe and pity as her older sister clawed her
way up through the fiercely competitive ranks of struggling models to achieve world-class status. She sincerely
admired Helen for enduring the stresses and brutal rig-
ours of maintaining herself at a constant peak of physical
perfection from the age of sixteen, when she had won
her first beauty competition, to her current graceful approach to thirty. But envy had no part in that admiration. Having seen the knife-edge of uncertainty on
which Helen's ego was constantly balanced, Honor had
pitied her with the complacency of someone who knew
how much of an illusion effortless beauty was, how false
the glamour of her world really was.

She looked down at the letter clenched in her hand.
No, she hadn't envied her sister at all.

Until now.

'Helen . . .' Her voice trailed off. Did she *really* want
to know? She gritted her teeth. She had no choice. He
was talking about meeting her, for goodness' sake!

'What?' Helen yawned again, stretching the tall, lithe
body, sculpted taut by diligent daily aerobics and rigid
dieting. Helen might eat at the best hotels, but she only
ever tasted their salads!

'Remember last time you stayed with me—you know
when we had the Valentine's Day Ball?' Honor had been
so busy helping to organise what was touted as being
the rural social event of the year that she had forgotten
to arrange a partner for herself and by then all her male
'mates' were spoken for. When Helen had arrived for
an unexpected few days' visit it had seemed a great idea
for her sister to use the extra ticket. Who better to help

create the necessary glitter for the event than a top international model?

'Mmm.' Helen sounded faintly wary, probably worried that Honor was going to request another charity appearance.

'Do you remember meeting anyone called Adam?' Honor held her breath, although she knew it was a forlorn hope. As soon as she had seen that wretched 'Helen' she had *known* ...

'Adam?' Her sister's vivid green eyes narrowed in thought, accentuating their perfect almond shape.

'Adam Blake.'

'Adam...Adam. No, I don't think so.' Helen shrugged cheerfully. 'You know what I'm like with names, darling.'

Honor did know. Unless people had the potential to be useful to her career Helen tended to operate on the principle out of sight, out of mind.

'Are you sure? Do moonlight and roses and ladies in distress ring any bells?' she persisted doggedly.

To her shock her sophisticated sister pinkened. Honor had never seen her blush before and now she knew why. That creamy pale, unmade-up skin flushed unevenly, in blotchy patches.

'Helen?' Her voice was sharper than she had intended. 'You *do* know who I'm talking about, don't you?'

'Not really. God, I'm dying for a coffee.'

'What does "not really" mean?' Honor scrambled up to follow her sister out into the tiny kitchen, watching with a jaundiced eye as Helen began puttering about on the bench-top. The only time her sister came even close to looking ungraceful was when she pretended to be domestic.

'It means that maybe I do and maybe I don't. I never asked who he was, although come to think of it he *might* have said that his name was Adam ...'

'*Who* said?'

'Just someone who helped me out that night. I got into an awkward situation and he happened along at the right time, that's all.'

That's *all*? Honor wasn't fooled by her sister's casualness.

It took another half-hour and two cups of bitter black coffee to extract the story from her sister, and it was every bit as painful as Honor had known it would be.

Some time just after midnight, Helen had got into an undignified tussle with an overheated and over-inebriated admirer whom her customary haughtiness had failed to freeze off. When she had ducked out of the hall to escape his attentions he had followed, leaping amorously upon her in the rose-garden, tearing the bodice of her dress just in time for some amateur celebrity-hunter with a camera to get a couple of supremely compromising shots.

Helen's unnamed gallant had not only appeared out of the darkness to haul the man off and send him smartly on his drunken way, but had driven her back to the cottage in her ruined dress and left her with the promise that he would make sure the photographs never saw the public light of day.

'I never said anything because I just wanted to forget the whole embarrassing incident,' said Helen sharply, forestalling Honor's obvious question. 'My dress was an Ungaro, you know. The shoulder-strap was practically torn away and though I got a dressmaker to repair it it was never quite the same. I was nearly in tears, I was so furious. I hardly spoke to your Adam, if that's who it was, except to give him directions to this place. I only went to that damned ball because of you, you know, and what did you do but go off and leave me to the mercy of some drunken moron!'

'I didn't abandon you—it was more like the other way around. I couldn't get close with all your admirers clustering around,' said Honor, stung by the unfairness of the accusation. 'Besides, you told me to keep my distance from you, remember, because I wasn't feeling very well and you had that Australian swimsuit shoot in a few days and didn't want to get my germs. In fact my infectiousness was the *supposed* reason for your suddenly rushing off to Sydney the next morning.'

'Yes, well, I wasn't going to hang around and wait for some sleazy tabloid to pick up on the story and ring me for a comment. Can you imagine the headline—TOP MODEL IN TOPLESS ROMP?' She shuddered. 'My publicist would have fits. Not to mention Mother.' Honor was unsurprised to note that her concern for their ambitious mother, who had been the driving force behind Helen's career and was still her manager, took second place to her fear of adverse publicity. Helen was always acutely conscious of her image, to the point of paranoia.

'He got a shot of you *topless*?' Her throaty voice squeaked with horror. She knew that her sister always turned down nude work—'preserving her mystique', she called it. Even swimsuit offers were accepted only when their prestige was exceptional.

'Well, it wasn't quite that bad,' Helen conceded grudgingly. 'But I was being considered for that new aerobics clothing line at the time and they wanted someone with a squeaky-clean image. I couldn't afford to risk even a mild scandal. Why all the interest now? Don't tell me this Adam is looking for me after all this time?'

No, but only because he already thought he had found her!

And because Honor always tried to live up to her name she had shown Helen her precious letters... all except the last few passionate epistles which she couldn't quite bring herself to share. It would be too much like a betrayal.

Her sister's reaction was quite predictable. She had given one or two a cursory read-through and collapsed in hilarity.

'He thinks you're me? What a hoot! He's in for a shock, isn't he?' she giggled with an adolescent glee that

Honor darkly thought ill befitted a woman who was almost thirty. 'Especially since his last sight of you was when you were snoring like a jet-engine!'

'Snoring?' Honor's puzzlement was shadowed by the gloomy presentiment of further humiliation.

'Drooling, too, as I recall,' Helen added with sisterly cruelty. 'I couldn't go back into the hall with my dress practically in shreds so we cut through the gardens to get to his car and there were you, parked on a bench like a homeless tramp. Since you'd said you were going to stay until the last gasp no matter how rotten you were feeling, I told what's-his-name to carry you to your car so that you wouldn't get double pneumonia or something if you didn't wake up for a while. I thought if I told him you were my sister he'd make a fuss and insist on you coming with me so I did us both a favour and told him you were a distant relative with an extremely jealous husband. I even left you the stolen roses that drunk tried to foist on me in order to keep my hands busy while he tried to have his sweaty way...'

'Thanks a million,' grumbled Honor, cringing at the unflattering picture she must have presented. She should never have taken those pain-killers on top of several glasses of champagne.

'What—what was he like? What did he say?'

In her mind she had pictured the man who wrote to her as being quiet and reassuringly ordinary-looking, with kind eyes and a ready smile. Socially unsophisticated. The kind of man who would be more interested in a woman's mind than her appearance. The kind who preferred warmth and humour to the cold perfection of glamour.

Helen was maddeningly vague. 'I can't remember. He was thin and dark...I think. He made the usual protective male noises but I didn't really listen. He must have been pretty strong, the way he carried you, but he drove some awful station wagon or something. Not my type at all!' It was typical of Helen to judge the man by his car. At Honor's sound of annoyance she said impatiently, 'Well, what do you *expect* me to say? He wasn't Superman. There was nothing memorable about him—not that I *wanted* to remember anything about the whole wretched business anyway. I'm swamped in gorgeous men every day of my working life, darling, why should I remember some unimportant stranger I met ages ago?'

Honor looked at the valentine—slightly dog-eared from months of affectionate handling—that had started it all, and sternly made herself face facts.

'He couldn't possibly have meant to write to me—not after having met you,' she sighed, far too aware of her sister's devastating tunnel-vision effect on men to have any illusions about how she rated in comparison.

'What does it matter who he *meant* to write to? It was you he ended up corresponding with,' Helen pointed out kindly, spoiling it by adding, 'If you ask me, he's got to be pretty arrogant in the first place if he thinks a woman like *me* would be interested in some country hick...'

'He doesn't live in the country, he lives in Auckland,' Honor automatically defended.

'Small-town hick, then,' said Helen, ignoring the fact that Auckland was New Zealand's largest city. She was very proud of the fact that she had outgrown her home country, whereas Honor had very proudly grown back into it after several years' enforced stay in the canyons of New York city.

'Anyway, it was a gross piece of assumption on his part that I'd be interested. I don't know what you're worrying about. If he dumps you what have you lost? Only another penfriend, for goodness' sake. You used to have stacks of them when you were twelve—I should have thought you'd have grown out of that sort of teenage stuff by now. Doesn't say much for your social life, does it? I *told* you burying yourself in this place would stunt your growth. I suppose, as usual, you let your imagination run away with you and built it into some grand romance in your mind.'

By now Helen was into full, condescending stride. She had never understood Honor's fascination with the written word, had pitied her for wasting her time reading about life instead of following her big sister's example and going out and actually *living* it.

'They're just *letters*, Honor, it's not as if he ever actually bothered to make the effort of meeting me—you— face to face,' she continued bracingly. 'And stop looking so guilty. The whole thing was his mistake in the first place for assuming that there was only one Miss Sheldon. Imagine thinking *I'd* enjoy writing letters to someone I don't even know!' She shuddered delicately. 'If I tried to answer every fan letter I get I'd never have time to do anything else. You know what I'm like—I don't even answer *yours* . . .'

Honor gave up trying to explain. Helen would never understand in a million years what those letters had meant to her. How much joy they had brought her, how deeply committed she had felt as she had progressively revealed more and more of her thoughts and feelings to a man she'd never met.

And what about those most recent letters she had sent? Honor went cold with horror at the thought of what she had ardently revealed. Talk about drooling! Oh, God, what a *mess* . . . !

She knew she couldn't just hang around waiting for the axe to fall. She couldn't stand the agony. And the thought of putting it all into writing was abhorrent. She couldn't present him such a shock in a letter, in cold black and white, with no opportunity for her to test his mood first for the best way to explain. Whatever the embarrassment to herself, she owed it to them both to talk to him in person. But how? If she wrote asking for a meeting without telling him why, he would still get an awful shock on seeing her. It would be far better if she could talk to him first on the phone—soften him up for the disappointment...

There lay the rub. Adam didn't usually bother to head his letters with any address and the recent letters hadn't even been dated. All she had to go on was the North Shore box number he had originally given her.

While Helen was upstairs packing the vast number of clothes she had brought for her few days' visit, Honor leafed through the telephone book with sweaty palms although she already knew what she would find: curiosity had tempted her to peep once before. There was no A. Blake in either the personal or business listings with an address on the North Shore.

This time, desperation led her to run through all the very numerous Auckland Blakes and at the very bottom of the alphabetical listings something jumped out at her.

Z. Blake, Arrow House, Blake Rd, Evansdale.

Honor blinked. Coincidence? A vague memory stirred and her thick brows drew together in an effort to bring it into focus. Hadn't she read in the local paper a few years ago about a local hero, Zachary Blake, who had made a fortune diversifying his family's citrus fruit orchard into production of avocados, kiwi fruit, nashi and other exotic and expensive fruits aimed at the overseas restaurant market? He had been one of the first 'Kiwi fruit millionaires' in the boom days before farmers all over the country started jumping on the exotic fruit bandwagon and he had used his wealth to diversify even further, into food processing and other related industries.

Might Adam be a relation of the Zachary Blakes? He had never mentioned having relatives who lived in her vicinity, but then she had never mentioned having a sister. Their letters had been for and about each other, a deliciously selfish and possessive indulgence that no one else was permitted to share.

But if Adam *was* a relative, even only a distant once, that might explain his presence at the Valentine Ball, since people in the area had been encouraged to sell tickets among their wider circle of families and friends. Perhaps the Evansdale Blakes could tell her how to get in touch with Adam. It was worth a try.

Never one to procrastinate, Honor made a furtive phone call to the number in the book, nervously aware that if Helen walked in and realised what she was doing she would probably earn herself another patronising sisterly lecture.

The discovery that Adam was not only known to the Evansdale Blakes but was actually in current residence with them shocked her into stammering confusion, especially when it became evident that unless she stated a very explicit purpose for her call she was not going to be put through to him. The sheer unexpectedness of it all caused her to hang up in a panic and only afterwards did she think it strange that the man had never bothered to ask her for her name and yet had seemed fixated on demanding to know what she wanted from Adam. The thought of having to ring back and humiliate herself by relating the ghastly mix-up to an unknown and obviously unsympathetic third party made up her mind. The direct approach was the only option left.

As soon as Helen wafted out the door in a cloud of L'Air du Temps, trilling farewells, Honor grimly wheeled her bicycle out of the shed. There was no point in trying to get any work done until she had done everything she could to talk to Adam.

In ordinary circumstances she would have enjoyed the bike ride, being quite used to the eccentricities of the dilapidated machine that she had bought from the previous owner of the house, along with all the other junk in the rusting corrugated-iron shed at the bottom of her garden. The Waitakere Ranges were a popular training ground for triathletes looking to build up their cycling stamina on the hilly terrain and although Honor was nowhere near their league, either in fitness or in the snazziness of their gear and complex machines, she shared their appreciation of a brisk workout along the quiet, winding, bush-lined country roads. This morning, however, an unexpected spring shower and the hollow nervousness in her empty stomach served to make her wish she had at least waited until after lunch to do her duty.

Consequently, by the time she arrived at the Blake house she had a very severe case of cold feet even before she saw its palatial splendour. Looking down at her mud-spotted shoes and stockings, she cursed herself for changing out of her jeans into a skirt and blouse but she had wanted to make a reasonable impression. Now her rain-damp skirt clung clammily to her legs, although thankfully her light jacket had protected her white blouse, which would probably have turned transparent. At least she had been bright enough to wear a scarf and she took it off now, running cold fingers through the tangled waves of her hair.

After wheeling her embarrassingly shabby bike a little way back down the road and parking it safely out of sight in the undergrowth, she advanced cautiously down the driveway, keeping close to the trees that lined one side, where the footing on the larger stones was easier for her smooth-soled flat shoes than the fine gravel at the centre. As she approached the wide front door Honor caught a glimpse of her reflection in one of the curtained windows and halted. Goodness, she looked like a tart with her skirt rucked up between her legs. Perhaps modesty would be better served by taking her stockings off. Her skirt would be less likely to stick to smooth, bare legs.

She made a smart about-turn on to a narrow paved pathway along the side of the house, looking around for some cover. There was a little thicket of low-growing shrubs next to a fishpond and she ducked in among them and crouched to peel off the damp stockings quickly. Unfortunately her bare feet sank into the loamy ground and she had to wipe them with her scarf before she could slide back into her shoes.

By the time she rose from the bushes Honor was flushed and thoroughly annoyed with herself for her uncharacteristic obsession with her appearance. What did it matter what she looked like? She wasn't Helen and that was all that would matter to Adam.

Unfortunately, just as she popped up a man suddenly appeared from the rear corner of the house, running directly towards her with such an implicit threat in the lean of his powerful body that Honor reacted to sheer instinct and began to run back towards the drive, unzipping her jacket to push the grubby stockings deep into the inside pocket as she did so. A garbled shout sent her deeper into panicked embarrassment and there were suddenly people running all over the place as she slammed into a brick wall with such force that she went sprawling backwards, her fingers trapped inside her pocket by the stretchy octopus her stockings had suddenly become.

'Look out, she's got a weapon!' she heard, before the brick wall reached down and hauled her up by the scruff of her jacket, one beefy hand punching down into her pocket, almost tearing it off as he wrestled her for her stockings and dragged them free.

Ears ringing, Honor was conscious of all the chaos around her coming to a dead stop as the limp trophy was dangled from her captor's hand.

'What the hell——?'

Honor looked up into the furious brown eyes of the menacingly big blond man who held her. He had shoulders like a rugby player and a broken nose to match and his grip on her jacket was so tight he was practically strangling her with the collar. Perversely, his rough treatment vanquished her embarrassed fright and ignited her temper.

'Let me go, you big, stupid oaf!' she hissed, writhing in his grasp and jarring her fists as she pounded them against his iron chest.

'No way,' he snarled, shaking her until her teeth rattled. 'What the hell were you going to do with these?' He dangled the stockings tauntingly in front of her pink nose and from the flash of yellow heat in the brown eyes she wondered whether he intended to strangle her with them. He certainly looked as if he'd like to, witnesses or no.

'Wear them on my head!' she snarled back with furious sarcasm. 'Or, better still, use them as a slingshot to crack that Neanderthal skull of yours!'

Dimly she heard the commotion re-start around her as several other men tried unsuccessfully to drag her out of the masher's bone-cracking grasp.

Amid the turmoil she heard the startling words which had the effect of freezing her share of the struggle.

'Police? You're *police*?' She cranked her head around, noticing that what had seemed like a crowd was only five men, all as big and brawny as the man who held her, and one woman who looked as if she could match them muscle for muscle.

She glared up at the man who still held her. 'What is this, a training exercise in police brutality? You know I could make a complaint about this!'

'You're the one who ran,' the blond giant ground out, unimpressed by her outrage.

'I didn't realise running was a criminal offence, Mr Plod,' she snapped back. 'If you've made a run in my stockings maybe I can have *you* arrested.'

A tiny snicker of inappropriate laughter from one of the men was quelled with a single look from the senior-ranking officer who now stepped forward to take charge.

'I'd like you to accompany me to the station, miss, to answer some questions——'

'I've got a few the little bitch can answer right now,' the man holding her cut in crudely. 'Who's in it with you?' he demanded savagely. 'Where's your accomplice? You must have one—you're too dumb to have hatched this on your own. Is he your lover?' He gave her body a contemptuous survey that took her in from head to battered toe. 'If he is, don't expect him to give a damn what happens to you now; I doubt if he thinks that a brown dumpling is worth doing hard time for— you'll be the one to take the fall——'

'Mr *Blake*——!' The senior officer again attempted to intervene. This time it was Honor who stopped him.

'Blake?' Shock was piling on shock from all directions. Her heart sank as she looked into the blazing brown eyes. 'Mr——? You—you're not a policeman? *You're* Zachary Blake?'

Colour raked along his tanned cheeks as if she had struck him a stinging blow. 'You know damned well who I am, you lying bitch——'

'That's enough, Mr Blake! You can let her go now. We have the situation under control.' The order came sharply, and this time the blond avenger reluctantly released her, stepping back and slowly flexing his big fists at his side as if imagining them squeezing around her neck.

Honor swallowed painfully. So much for the subtle approach!

'I—don't know what this is about. I'm just here to see your...to see Adam Blake...' she offered tentatively, realising that she didn't know what relationship he had to this man.

Instead of soothing him, her timid foray into explanation prompted a searing explosion of curses that followed her all the way to one of the unmarked police cars at the back of the house into which she was rapidly hustled.

'You don't understand,' she cried, as they pressed her into the back seat. 'Please, let me speak to Adam, he'll know who I am!'

'And how well do you know him?' queried the senior officer in a strange voice as the policewoman slid alongside Honor from the opposite door.

Honor felt a tiny glimmer of hope that she could salvage herself from this comedy of errors. 'Very well,' she said firmly. 'Just ask him about our letters. Tell him that my name is Sheldon!'

'*Our* letters?' He pounced on what he evidently saw as a discrepancy. 'Is Sheldon your surname? And what is your first name, Ms Sheldon?'

She hesitated, disturbed by the sudden silky smoothness with which he spoke. 'Helen.'

Guilty colour flooded her face, but she reasoned that, once Adam had vouched for the name, then she could set about putting her identity right.

But her brief flirtation with dishonesty cost her dearly, because the policeman turned away from the open car door and addressed someone behind him with sardonic humour. 'Hear that, Adam? She says you know each other well. Says that her name is Helen Sheldon. Care to give us a formal ID for the report?'

'Sure.' A backlit figure moved around and ducked down to look into the car, and Honor gasped as she saw his face.

'No. That's definitely not Helen Sheldon. I've never seen this woman before in my life.'

The man that she had thought was Zachary Blake followed up his icy denial with a venomous smile that twisted his mouth from snarl to sneer.

'Calling you dumb was an understatement. Didn't it enter your tiny mind that it might seem a trifle suspicious to claim to know me at the same time that you were busy trying to pretend that you thought I was my own brother? Or maybe you're being very, very clever. Maybe you're looking ahead to a defence of mental incompetence. Don't bank on it. Even if this turns out to be the bumbling amateur farce it looks to be I'm going to make sure that the case against you is nailed down tight. As far as I'm concerned people like you are the lowest scum on earth!'

And with that Adam Blake slammed the door and stalked off, leaving Honor in the ruins of her shattered dreams.

That Neanderthal thug, that—that rough, crude, bullying *pig* was her delightful, passionate, poetic, ideal man? Impossible!

If anyone was laying claim to a false identity, it was Adam Blake!

CHAPTER THREE

Assisting the police with their enquiries while trying to retain at least a modicum of personal privacy was hard work, Honor decided wearily that evening as she made herself a solitary dinner.

Three hours! It had taken *three hours* in that police station to satisfy grim officialdom that she wasn't a homicidal maniac with a lethal grudge against the Blake family!

Of course, it hadn't helped that she had not been carrying a skerrick of personal identification, but, as she had pointed out to the slit-eyed Gibbon, handbags were notoriously difficult to juggle on the handlebars of a bicycle! And then there had been the complication of trying to explain her actions without compromising Helen. The police were quite capable of arranging for her sister to be detained at the airport if they thought Honor's story required her corroboration. Helen would be livid if that happened.

Unfortunately, after she had down-played the whole thing by treating it as a joke, claiming that she had known all along that Adam had been writing to the wrong sister but had decided it was time to 'fess up, the DI had insisted on driving her home and viewing the physical evidence for himself.

Then, instead of just glancing at *one* of the letters, he had read the entire batch, an invasion of privacy that Honor had endured only because she suspected that he would be happy to produce a search warrant and go through the whole house if she said no.

'You don't mind if I borrow this one for a little while, do you?' he had murmured at last, not bothering to wait for her answer as he had tucked the piece of evidence complacently into his jacket pocket. Naturally it was one of Adam's steamier efforts and Honor had cringed on his behalf. If he became a police-station joke he would never forgive her. Not that he was likely to now, anyway.

Honor sighed as she ate the desiccated omelette she had overcooked in her distraction. At least there was one consolation. She had achieved what she had set out to do that morning. By now Adam Blake must be fully aware of who she was... and who she *wasn't*.

Instead of softening the blow, she had managed to deliver him a real pile-driver!

Another consolation was awaiting her in the refrigerator: a beautifully rich chocolate cake made for her by one of the group of little old ladies among whom she circulated copies of the talking books that she recorded for the Blind Institute.

She cut herself a bigger than usual slice and retreated to her lounge to enjoy the last rays of the sun stretching into the small, north-facing room, sprawling on the carpet by the French doors and turning the stereo up as loud as was comfortable, the poignant, meditative mood of Elgar's cello concerto perfectly suiting her frame of mind.

Halfway through the concerto her chronically bad-tempered cat, Monty, stalked into the room and availed himself of the last crumbs of cake on the plate before mercilessly clawing a comfortable position in the centre of her supine body, his wheezing, rumbling purr providing a monotonous counterpoint to Sir Edward's masterly composition.

So loud, in fact, was the music and Monty's vibrating bass that Honor didn't hear the bell or the knocking on her distant front door and it was only when the French doors behind her head rattled violently that she realised she had a visitor.

She jerked upright, shrieking as Monty dug his claws through her faded shirt into her skin and hung on grimly as she scrambled to her feet. She staggered to undo the tricky door-catch, at the same time trying to brush off the hugely outraged fluffy burr adhering to her sagging clothes.

The tussle ended when the door flew open under intense pressure from without and Monty, scrabbling for purchase against Honor's chest, sprang at the interloper's head and rebounded off it into the relative safety of the darkness beyond.

'What the *hell*——?'

Honor didn't need to open her pained eyes to recognise her cursing visitor. He had greeted her before with that same expression, uttered in that very same, furious tone of voice.

Adam Blake. In black trousers and a black fisherman's sweater and with a dark scowl on his tanned face he looked larger than ever, and menacingly attractive. The high, hard cheekbones and strong jaw gave him a sculpted male beauty that she had barely registered during their last hasty confrontation. He and Helen would make a striking pair, Honor realised drearily. They were two of a kind, blessed with golden good looks and a physical magnetism that was impossible to ignore.

'I—I'm sorry.' To her horror she realised there was a small trickle of blood oozing down his temple and she instantly forgot the stinging on her own chest. 'It—it was only my cat...'

'If that's your cat I'd hate to see your dog!' Adam swiped at the trickle with the back of a big hand and Honor winced in sympathy.

'I don't have a dog——'

'With a pit-bull like that for a cat I don't suppose you need one.'

Honor's heart began to settle back into a more normal rhythm. 'You startled him, that's all. He was scared and you were standing between him and freedom.' She automatically searched in her jeans pocket for a crumpled handkerchief which she apologetically held out to him. 'Here, you're still bleeding——'

He ignored the pacifying gesture, producing a handkerchief of his own, a crisp white square, beautifully ironed, with which he dabbed his temple. 'If you'd turn that bloody noise down you might hear your doorbell!'

Honor bristled as she did so. 'That *noise* happens to be Elgar,' she said tartly, when she had quietened the stereo. 'I thought you liked classical music.'

His eyes narrowed at the familiarity implicit in the comment. They weren't so much brown as blond, Honor thought inconsequently, a shade or so deeper than the dark honey hair.

'Where are they?'

'They? There's no one here but me,' Honor blurted, and then wondered whether she had made a mistake in admitting she was alone to a furiously angry man. 'Mr Blake——'

'Mr Blake?' His blond eyebrows raked sardonically upwards. 'Why so formal all of a sudden? What happened to "you big oaf" and "Neanderthal"... *darling*?'

The snarled endearment was definitely a threat. Freshly conscious of his solidity and size, Honor swallowed, bravely standing her ground as she nervously tucked a strand of hair behind her left ear. 'I—I suppose you've spoken to that detective——'

'We had a fascinating conversation. Now where are they?'

'W-who?'

'Not who, what! And don't bother running that doe-eyed-innocence routine past me; I don't buy it. If you don't start co-operating I'll have you slapped behind bars so fast your head will spin!'

No need—it was spinning wildly already. Doe-eyed? No one had ever called her that before. If it hadn't been yelled with such insulting emphasis she might have mistaken it for a compliment.

'The police are perfectly satisfied that I had nothing to do with...to do with whatever trouble you're in!' Honor said stiffly, resisting the urge to shout back. She wished she knew what she was defending herself against. Exactly what she had been suspected of had never been precisely defined. All she knew was that it involved a serious threat, and that there would be dire consequences for herself if she so much as breathed a word of the case to anyone until cleared to do so by the police.

'It's not I that's in the most trouble right now,' he grated. 'If you don't produce those letters in the next five minutes I'll tear this place apart myself.'

'The letters?' Honor almost wilted in relief. 'What do you want them for?'

'What do you think?'

He took a step towards her and Honor put a defensive hand against the front of her shirt and was disconcerted to feel bare skin. She looked down. To her horror Monty's hind legs had done a very good job of dragging most of her buttons out of their worn buttonholes. Her faded shirt had parted over her breasts, revealing a similarly shabby bra, one she had hung on to long past its prime because it was so comfortable.

She gasped, and hastily began rebuttoning, freezing as Adam suddenly reached forward and pulled one side of her shirt out of her hand. While she stood, stiff with shock, he lifted his other hand and ran blunt square fingers over the tender flesh swelling above the frayed lace. A sharp sting made her wince as his thumb dragged in the wake of his fingers.

'It seems your pet is fairly indiscriminate in his victims—you're bleeding as much as I am. You ought to get something on those scratches straight away; the skin on your breasts is a lot more delicate and susceptible to damage than the skin on exposed parts of the body.'

His lack of embarrassment only made Honor's more acute as his hand slowly withdrew, leaving behind a tingling awareness of his touch.

Bewildered by such consideration in the midst of his raging fury, and guilty that she had suspected him, even for a moment, of carnal motives, Honor's eyes flicked to the vivid, red-beaded line down the side of his face.

'I-I have some antiseptic ointment in the bathroom if you want some...' she offered, clutching the front of her shirt and nervously backing away.

Something feral gleamed deep in the golden eyes. 'Good idea. Why don't you go and get it and we can tend to each other's wounds?'

Have him touch her breasts again with that strange, gentle insistence? Honor could feel her face heat up as she turned and fled for the bathroom. After all the trouble she had gone to to dress up nicely for him earlier, he had to walk in on her when she was clad in scruffy jeans and a shirt she had picked up in a jumble sale!

Only two of the four scratches she had sustained were seeping blood but Honor cleaned and applied the cream to all of them. She didn't want to give Adam the excuse of demanding an inspection, and the ruthless satisfaction on his face when she had begun to blush had told her that he had instantly perceived her physical awareness of his masculinity as a weakness that could be exploited to his advantage.

Remember the letters, she told herself severely as she tucked her shirt firmly back into her jeans. Adam Blake is not really the snarling, aggressive, insulting bully he appears to be. He is a warm, charming, sensitive man who just happens to be justifiably confused at the moment. Grabbing the tube of ointment, she kept repeating the incantation as she went back to face him.

The warm, charming and sensitive man was sitting behind her desk rifling through the drawers. His concern had been merely a ploy to get her out of the room, she realised with an acute sense of betrayal.

'Hey, what do you think you're doing?'

He ignored her, bending in the chair to pull out another drawer, and tip out its contents on the floor. Realising that she had no hope of physically stopping him, Honor tried to use sweet reason.

'Mr—Adam, if you want those letters back I'll be happy to give them to you. I know you're angry but truly, I had no idea that you thought you were writing to my sister—how could I? You wrote to this address and I'm the only H. Sheldon who lives here. I didn't even know that you and Helen had met—I thought you just must have seen me at the ball and...and...'

His head lifted, his eyes chilly with contemptuous disbelief. 'Found you so instantly and devastatingly attractive that I couldn't forget you?' Honor blushed painfully as her foolish fantasies were stripped to their unlikely origins. 'Yes, I can see how often that must happen to you.' His sarcasm was as glacial as his stare.

'Perhaps that's how you get your kicks—by enticing strange men to write to you under false pretences. Do you advertise in the personal columns, too, and send your gullible prospects a photograph of your beautiful sister to stimulate their interest? Are you so jealous of her that in some sick and twisted way you try to *be* her——?'

'I'm perfectly happy being myself! You seem to be forgetting that *you're* the one who made the approach to *me*,' Honor flung at him, mortified by his interpretation of her character. 'All I did was innocently answer a card that *I* received——'

'You have an interesting interpretation of innocence,' Adam rapped out. 'The police tell a different version...the one about how you thought it was great fun to lead me on until you decided I was becoming too persistent, an embarrassing annoyance, and thought it was time to front up and deliver the punch line in person.'

Oh, damn! She knew that somehow her lies would return to haunt her.

'I only said that because I was trying to keep Helen out of it. I didn't want the police involving her in any awkward publicity——' she protested.

'But she *is* involved, isn't she, right up to her beautiful neck?' he cut in savagely. Honor could practically *see* his wounded male pride throbbing. 'I suppose she was in on the joke, too?'

'There wasn't any joke.' Honor stared him straight in the eye, willing him to believe her. 'I didn't realise what had been going on myself until I was reading one of your letters this morning and...well, of course I showed them to Helen straight away and she told me about what you did for her at the ball, and then I knew...'

'You *showed* her?' Adam's voice rose sharply in conjunction with his powerful body as he came sweeping to his feet. 'Helen's *here*?'

The flare of anticipation that glowed momentarily in his eyes said it all. The beauteous Helen would be forgiven her transgressions whereas her plain, unprepossessing sister would not. Honor felt a little kick of malicious temper. If he could be insensitive so could she.

'Not now, no. She *was* staying with me for a few days, but she flew to Sydney this afternoon. When I told her about the mix-up she wasn't really interested. She doesn't answer fan letters, you see, so she probably would never have written to you even if you *had* sent your letters to the right address in New York.'

Instead of flinching Adam fixed her with a drilling look. 'Something else you lied to the detective inspector about? You told him your sister was in New York——'

'I didn't lie, I said she *lives* in New York, not that she was there right at this moment——'

'A lie by implication is no less a lie,' said Adam grimly. 'You seem to make a habit of taking advantage of other people's mistakes, don't you, Honor? Quite the little opportunist, in fact. I wonder what else you're hiding...?'

With that he sat back down and continued his search, his careless violation of her tidy drawers a deliberate goad to which Honor instinctively responded. She marched around the desk and pulled open the bottom drawer. She took out the stack of letters that the detective had put back in meticulous order and dumped them in front of him.

'There! Satisfied?'

He was shuffling impatiently through them. 'Not nearly. I don't care about these. Where are the others?'

'What others?'

'You know very well. The ones I *didn't* send.'

Honor stared at his gritty profile, wondering whether the blow from Monty's claws could have caused a mild concussion in so hard a head. Now she looked more closely she could see the fine tension lines radiating out around his mouth and eyes, signs of powerful emotions kept in rigid check. He looked like a man at the very edge of his control. What anger he had released so far was merely the tip of the iceberg.

'They're all there,' she said warily, feeling like a passenger on the *Titanic*. 'Except for the one that the detective took with him, of course...'

'And you can thank God that he handed it back to me instead of filing it as evidence,' he growled, and suddenly she thought she understood. He wanted reassurance that she hadn't showed the most revealing letters to anyone else.

'Look——' She reached for the envelopes and yelped as her hand was slapped down on to the desk under a savage paw. 'I was only going to show you,' she said reproachfully. 'If you're talking about the last few letters they're right here, at the back. See?' She showed him with her free hand.

'Matching envelopes,' he said cryptically as he checked the contents. 'Hide them in plain sight. Clever.'

The press of his encompassing palm loosened over hers but just as she slid her flattened fingers gratefully free he curled his hand around her wrist and jerked her closer. Sitting down he was still almost as tall as she was standing. His voice was silky with cold menace. 'Now, be a good girl and show where you've hidden the others. If you give them to me we'll call it quits—after you've answered one or two pressing questions...'

She didn't like the sound of that. 'I don't know what you're talking about; there *are* no others.' She strained away from him while trying not to let the extent of her panic show. Maybe Adam Blake had a split personality; maybe his letters had been dictated by a separate persona that he wasn't consciously aware existed.

'If that's the way you want to play it.' The smile he gave her sent a chill up her spine. It was almost as if he relished her resistance.

'I'm not *playing*.' But he was... playing her straining body like a fish on a line, reeling her slowly in between his splayed knees with a gradually increasing pressure of her captured wrist.

'However many letters you might have posted, those are all that arrived here,' she told him, her normally rich, warm voice reedy with rising hysteria. How did you reason with a madman? 'Why don't you let me go and we can have a drink and talk about this sensibly?' Maybe alcohol was a bad idea. It might feed his paranoia. 'Or a cup of tea. That scratch is probably throbbing by now. Why don't you let me clean it for you and——? Oh!' With a slight flick of his wrist he brought her down on her knees, his thighs levering shut on either side of her torso. She gasped at the ruthless compression of her ribs, her hands pushing helplessly against the thick muscles bunching under the dark trousers.

He watched her twist and struggle in silence for a moment or two and then he leaned forward and cupped her pale face in his big hands with a tenderness that terrified her far more than his anger.

'Forget the tea and sympathy—I want something much more valuable. Would you like me to hurt you, Honor?'

His thumbs stroked behind her ears, his fingers threading up under her hair, cradling her skull, making her aware of its mortal fragility.

'Is that the only way I can make you tell the truth? The things about yourself you told me in your letters— I don't suppose *all* of them were lies. I remember you telling me once that you have a low pain threshold...' The slightly calloused edge of the outside of his palm lifted her jaw, stretching her soft throat uncomfortably taut. 'Shall we test the veracity of that statement first...?'

'Adam, please——'

His thumbs shifted to press across her trembling mouth. 'Don't beg yet, I haven't started.' His fingers massaged her scalp gently and suddenly black dots were dancing in front of Honor's eyes that had nothing to do with pain. After a shattering day this emotional overload was just too much.

'You're being totally unreasonable,' she whispered.

'And you don't think I have a right to be? I don't give in to blackmail. Not ever. I don't know how you got hold of those damned letters but if you thought you could use them against me you made a bad mistake——'

'But you *know* how I got them...you sent them to me!' The black dots had become red and Honor could hear the blood pounding in her ears. If he leaned any closer he would be kissing her. Or, more likely, biting...

'Did you think you'd get money for them? From me? Or are you more ambitious? Did you think you could use them to advance your journalistic career by flogging them off to the highest bidder? Maybe it was just malice. You wanted to make me pay for the sin of having wanted your sister instead of you. There are plenty of motives to choose from, aren't there?'

His breath was hot against her face. 'I—I'm not that kind of reporter,' she said weakly.

'You admitted you work for a newspaper.'

God, he was persistent. He somehow must have gained access to the record of her interview. How wonderful to have influence!

'Only part-time. I help produce the small local bi-weekly give-away. All very innocuous—flower shows, pony club meets, advertising supplements, that sort of thing. I do the layout on my computer. I have a desk-top publishing programme...'

Except for the shrunken omelette, she hadn't eaten anything but a breakfast slice of toast and now her blood sugar plummeted to her toes. What little colour there was left in her face drained away. Her eyes drifted defensively closed and she sagged as a wave of faintness passed over her.

She was barely aware of his hands sliding down to replace the pressure of his thighs against her waist, holding her limp body upright as he demanded insistently, 'And that's how you support yourself? Pay for this house, your car, your living expenses, clothes? By working part-time?'

He made it sound as if she lived high on the hog, instead of quietly and, for the most part, frugally. 'I— I do other things sometimes—voice commercials, for radio and television, leaflet layouts for people...' If she stopped fighting and answered his ridiculous questions maybe he would go back where he came from. Right now, that was all she wanted: to be left alone to crawl into bed and escape the bitter disillusionments of the day. 'The house was a gift from Helen. The car is six years old. I buy my clothes at sales. OK?'

'And you're an ardent conservationist?'

This new tangent bewildered her more than ever. Reluctantly Honor opened her heavy eyelids. Funny how secure she felt in his hold when only a few moments before it had been a merciless threat. 'I think whales are worth saving. Why? Don't you?'

'Not at the expense of human life,' he said, watching some of the colour slowly returning to her face as she frowned, the stern tilt of her thick straight eyebrows cancelling out the slightly dazed softness of her grey-green eyes.

Sullen-faced she had the look of a boy, all freckles and bony angles, but they were fine bones and the voice that came out of that neat, narrow mouth was anything but boyish. It was smooth and soft as velvet, as unexpectedly sensuous as the extravagant curves of her breasts and hips. He tightened his grip on her waist, unable to encircle the soft indentation even with his long fingers fully extended to the limit of their generous reach. It was a timely reminder that he liked his women tall and athletic like himself, narrow-hipped, supple and slender. And, more importantly, trustworthy.

'I don't think I've ever heard of whales harpooning fishermen,' Honor said, disliking the brooding shift of his expression.

'No, but there are radicals who would like to make their point just as graphically: vandalism, car bombs, threats to spike the products of companies they say exploit animals for profits with poison . . .'

Something in the way he said it made Honor stiffen. 'Is that what the police are investigating?' Her heart went out to him, until she realised what he was thinking. It was like a reviving dash of cold water in her face. 'My God, you can't think that *I* would have anything to do with it? For goodness' sake, you know me better than that!'

'On the contrary, I don't know you at all,' he corrected her coldly.

'Yes, you do. You have all my letters,' Honor insisted.

'And you have mine.'

She sighed. 'We're just going around in circles here. Look, I'm a pacifist, I have nothing but contempt for people who use violence to promote their point of view. I'm sorry you're having problems but they're nothing to do with me. I don't know what more I can say to convince you. Can't we talk about this tomorrow? I'm very tired. I've been man-handled, interrogated, frightened and insulted. Don't you think that's enough for one day?' Self-pity overwhelmed her as she catalogued her woes. And she hadn't even mentioned the worst shock of all: the defection of the romantic hero of her imagination!

'So am I. Tired of deception and evasion.' Adam stood, towering over her kneeling figure for a moment before making a rough sound of impatience and reaching down to lift her into the chair he had just vacated. 'But by all means let's talk about it tomorrow. In fact, now I think of it, that's an excellent idea. Why don't you just sit here and rest while I get your things?'

'My things?' She was talking to his back as he strode out of the room. 'What do you mean, get my things? Hey, where do you think you're going?'

Everywhere, it seemed. 'Getting her things' translated as conducting a rapid search of the rest of her house, ignoring Honor as she trailed furiously in his wake, protesting every step of the way.

'If this is the way you carry on, no wonder someone's threatening you!' she threw at him as he inspected the contents of the chest of drawers in her bedroom. 'It's a wonder no one brained you before now. And put that down! How dare you put your grubby paws on my underwear? If you don't get out of here right this minute I'm calling the police!'

It was an empty threat. The last thing she wanted after today was another run-in with authority, and Adam seemed to know it. He merely turned, a pair of plain white cotton panties strung from his tanned fingers.

'If you wear underwear like this I doubt you have to worry about it being pawed. Queen Victoria would definitely approve.'

Sarcastic beast! She whipped out some sarcasm of her own.

'What are you, an expert? I suppose you'll be raiding women's clothes-lines next. Why should we dress like tarts just to pander to your sleazy male fantasies? And what I wear under my clothes is none of your business, thank you very much!'

Thank God he had skipped the top right-hand drawer.

Unfortunately, even as she sent up the grateful prayer, he remedied the omission. He stilled, staring down at the contents, then lifted his head to cast a taunting glance at her fiery face as he deliberately, slowly, stirred the frothy, multi-coloured confection of lace until a violet satin suspender spilled over the edge and dangled provocatively into space, swinging like a brazen pendulum measuring out each long second of her embarrassment. She lifted her chin and set her mouth, her hands clenching at her sides.

He didn't say anything as he tucked it back. He didn't have to. His smirking expression said it all. First he made slighting remarks about her everyday underwear just because it was practical, and now he made her feel as if possession of a few feminine fripperies were a criminal offence! Oh, why had she made that smart remark about sleazy fantasies? She might have known the wretched man wouldn't overlook anything. Didn't the fact that he dotted every 'i' and crossed every 't' in his letters tell her anything?

'At the moment *everything* about you is my business,' he continued as if the silent interchange hadn't occurred. He opened her wardrobe and hauled out a soft suitcase he found on the top shelf, and began tossing in random pieces of clothing from hangers and drawers. 'By the time I've finished with you I'm going to know you better than you know yourself.'

'What are you doing? Stop that!' For a big man he was very quick on his feet, keeping his broad back to her and side-stepping each time she tried to move around him. He even raked a collection of cosmetics off her dressing-table into the gaping bag. 'Adam, I'm warning you——' She squeaked as he grabbed a blind handful from the top right-hand drawer and stuffed it into the bag. 'If you don't stop right now I'll—I'll——'

He zipped up the suitcase and turned so swiftly that she staggered back. 'You'll what?'

She frowned as she tried to think of a threat big enough to scare him. 'I'll call my lawyer.'

Some threat. Perhaps he guessed that she didn't have a lawyer.

'Fine. Call him from my phone,' he said coolly, taking her elbow in a light but numbing grip that had all her nerve-ends screaming to obey him. 'It's tapped but then no doubt, in view of your claim of complete innocence, you won't mind the police listening in.'

His phone? At last Honor forced herself to concede that he was not just trying to frighten her. He was succeeding!

'I'm not going anywhere with you.' Her feet contradicted her feeble protest as she trotted helplessly alongside him, steered by that implacably gentle, fingertip control.

She remembered now that he had mentioned in one of his letters that he had studied some obscure oriental form of self-defence in his teens and twenties. He probably knew pressure holds that would turn a six-foot body-builder into an obedient wimp, let alone a five-foot-three female of doubtful fitness. And she had fondly imagined he had engaged in the sport to compensate for an inferior physique, to bolster his self-confidence as a man. This man had self-confidence oozing out of every pore!

Back in the living-room he put down the suitcase, but not her arm, as he slotted the bolt on the French doors into place and turned to check the windows. 'Where are your keys?'

'On the hall table,' Honor blurted out automatically before finding the energy to struggle briefly as he swept her towards the door. 'You can't be serious about this——'

'I'm always serious.' That was a lie; many of his letters had been deliciously light-hearted.

'But—this is ridiculous.'

'I'm not leaving you here. Not until I'm sure where you fit in——'

'I don't fit in anywhere!' Honor wailed, as he scooped up her house-keys and hustled her out of her front door on to the uneven paved pathway.

'Until I know that for certain I'm not taking any chances. I can't afford to. There's too much at stake. Not just my personal safety or that of my family, but of other people, too. Maybe you really do have no connection with the extortion; maybe you are just a rotten coincidence,' he said, pocketing the keys after locking the door. 'But whether it was planned or not you're another source of pressure when I least need it, another distraction when I need to focus all my concentration and devote all my resources to my primary problem. At least if I know where you are I won't have to worry about what you're up to.

'And besides,' he said, as he opened the door of the sleek Mercedes parked outside her dainty white picket fence and pushed her into the back seat, along with her suitcase, 'if you *are* as innocent as you claim, has it occurred to you that by admitting an association with me you might have admitted yourself to a share of my danger? You could be a target for the fanatics, too, if they get the idea that they can hurt me by hurting you. If so you'll be safer where there's plenty of security.'

'Oh, so now this abduction is for *my* sake?' Honor said sullenly, to hide the shiver of fear that his words invoked.

She didn't doubt that Adam believed what he was saying. The frustration and bitterness in his voice expressed the rage of unaccustomed helplessness. She could see that he hated being a victim. By seizing control of her, he was regaining for himself a small measure of his power to control events around him.

He looked down at her grimly.

'You doubt me?' He unhooked a slim black folding cell-phone from his black belt and flipped it open, punching in some numbers.

He rose to his full height, carrying on a muttered conversation she couldn't hear properly before bending down and thrusting the phone towards her. 'Take it.'

She did, gingerly. 'Hello?'

'Detective Inspector Malcolm Marshall here, miss...'

Honor listened in silence as her former interrogator confirmed Adam's view, albeit in a considerably watered-down version!

'The threats that Mr Blake has received have been so general in nature that I can't say categorically that you're *not* in any danger whatsoever. However, neither can I say there is any positive indication you are. Therefore any sensible precaution you took to lower your profile for a little while wouldn't go amiss. I know Mr Blake would feel personally responsible if anything untoward *did* happen and in the circumstances I think his suggestion that you share his security arrangements is a sound and rather generous gesture....'

'Nice to have influence in high places!' Honor muttered as she handed the phone back, sensing from the amiable casualness with which Adam delivered his thanks and ended the call that all that official waffling had been something of a snow-job.

He shut the door with a very definitive clunk and slid into the seat in front of her, not even bothering to deny it. 'Yes, it is; that's why I use it.'

An automatic desire to puncture that smugness made Honor begin to scrabble at the nearest door-handle just as Adam hit the central-locking button.

'Don't bother, the rear doors are fitted with baby-locks,' he said, turning on the lights and engine. 'You don't have to panic. Marshall's a professional—and a damned good cop. He's not going to risk a high-flying career by laying himself open to a charge of misuse of police powers. He wouldn't lie to you, not even for me.

But he's perfectly happy to endorse an idea that makes his job easier . . . the fewer people running around loose on this case, the less chance there is of an information leak that might jeopardise a quick arrest.'

Honor scowled, instinctively prepared to believe him, even when he added coldly, 'As far as I'm concerned you can think of it as a form of protective custody. I still want some answers out of you and when I've got this other business out of the way I'm going to get them! Now stop bleating and do up your seatbelt.'

Honor obeyed, almost relieved to succumb to another wave of tiredness as Adam set the car in motion. Maybe he was right. Maybe tomorrow the personal antagonism that the upheavals of the day had caused to flare between them would have died down enough to clear up the misunderstanding with a simple explanation.

And if not, at least after a good sleep she would feel refreshed enough to renew the fight on a more even footing. She would just slug doggedly away until she rammed it through that thick skull that she was exactly who and what she said she was. It might take a while, as he threatened, but at least she would have the pleasure of a grovelling apology to look forward to when he finally—— An awful thought suddenly occurred to her.

'Wait a moment! Oh, no! *Stop the car!*' The seatbelt nearly cut her in half as her shriek of panic led Adam to jam the brake to the floor. As she choked and gasped and rubbed her scratched and sore chest it occurred to Honor that his instant reaction to her frantic command had been a bizarre act of trust in someone he mightily distrusted.

He swivelled in his seat to look at her. 'What's the matter? Are you all right?' he asked sharply, and she wished that she could afford to bask in that concern. But she knew it wouldn't last.

'Monty. He hates being alone and he's quite capable of running away if he thinks I've gone off and left him.' She watched fatalistically as the concern metamorphosed into fury. 'He might get killed on the road or poisoned by possum-bait or something. If you don't bring him with us I'm going to scream blue murder and fight like fury all the way. I'm not leaving here without my cat!'

CHAPTER FOUR

FOR the second time in twenty-four hours Honor found herself faced with the elegant grandeur of the Blake house. Discreet floodlighting of the two-storeyed, white-painted wooden façade made it even more intimidating by night than it had been earlier.

Reluctantly she opened the car door and stepped out on to the gravel, clutching the cardboard pet-carrier which bulged and rocked to its occupant's futile assault.

You and me both, Monty, she thought wryly as a savage yowl of frustration reverberated inside the carton and the driver of the car slammed his door with an expressive force before striding around to the boot to remove her suitcase.

'Well, what are you waiting for?' Adam growled, moving up beside her. He had subjected her to a blistering silence during the ride over, and the one time that she had tried to break the tension she had blundered disastrously.

She had tentatively asked how Zachary Blake and his family were going to react to the added burden of an unexpected guest at this awkward time.

'Is that supposed to be some kind of tasteless joke?' he'd lashed back coldly.

'I—no——' she'd stammered, thinking that nothing about the man seemed simple or straightforward.

'You expect me to believe that you don't know that Zach is dead?'

'*Dead*?' Honor was shocked. Her voice had dropped to a sepulchral whisper as she'd pondered the horrendous possibilities in the light of the current situation.

'My God, you mean—*murdered*?'

'No, I don't mean murdered,' Adam had said through clenched teeth. 'My brother died of an embolism three months ago.'

'Oh... I'm very sorry... I didn't know.' Honor had looked away from his angry face, memories of the grief she had suffered after her father's death three years ago flooding through her and bringing with it understanding.

She had done quite a few irrational things herself in the weeks after her bluff and cheerful father's fatal stroke, before time had begun its healing work and restored her emotional equilibrium. Might not the same kind of thing have happened to Adam? The timing of those love-letters was about right. Had grief over his brother's death caused him to behave with an uncharacteristic recklessness that he was now bitterly regretting?

'Since the newspaper you help produce ran a rather large obituary at the time I find that very difficult to believe.' His cutting answer had interrupted her sympathetic musing and she'd compressed her lips to control the impulse to slice back. He had every right to be angry if he genuinely thought that she had been pretending ignorance for some obscure motive of her own.

'It was probably while I was away on holiday. I spent a couple of weeks skiing in Queenstown about then.'

His grunt could have been one of acceptance or disbelief so she'd added pointedly, 'In fact, I remember writing to you on the monogrammed notepaper of the hotel I was staying at, so it would be easy enough to check the dates——' She'd stopped as she realised that she was assuming that her letters to him had been as cherished as his to her. For all she knew he might have thrown them away as soon as he had read them. The thought had made her dwindle in her seat.

He hadn't even grunted that time. He'd merely glared out into the headlit ribbon of road unwinding out of the darkness. The subject was closed and she'd sensed that any attempt to continue it would be just as rigidly ignored. The barrier of his anger was impenetrable. He fiercely resented the fact that she knew things about him that he didn't want her—hadn't intended her—to know, intimate thoughts that were more easily written than spoken. The connection established through their letters wasn't a bond as far as he was concerned, it was a choke-chain, a humiliating shackle that would inhibit him every time he looked at her.

Her eyes had fallen to his big hands effortlessly controlling the steering-wheel and she'd winced at the scratches that now adorned the hard knuckles. Monty had not taken kindly to being placed in confinement. He had stiffened his splayed legs and fought every inch of the way. Even while Adam had cursed and sworn to wring the animal's ungrateful neck she noticed that he had handled him as gently as the slashing claws would allow. She wondered sourly if he would have been as restrained in his handling if *she* had bitten and scratched and physically fought the imposition of his will. She had a feeling not!

For the rest of the journey she had brooded on that galling inequity.

She looked at Adam now as he stood before her on the gravelled driveway—big, impatient, arrogantly domineering. Actually he and Monty had an awful lot in common, she thought acidly. They were both extremely stubborn, they objected violently to opposition and on encountering it displayed a sad tendency to lash out at the nearest handy target.

'I was just wondering whether another policeman was going to come barrelling out of the shrubbery at me,' Honor lied, unwilling to admit that one of the reasons she was hanging back was because she felt nervous at what she was going to find inside the house. Would she face more hostility and suspicion? Who were the inhabitants and what, if anything, had Adam told them about her?

'In other words you want to know what our security arrangements are,' he said caustically. 'Forget it. I'm not *that* stupid!'

'Really? That's funny—you certainly give that impression!' Honor snapped back, stung by the fresh evidence of his mistrust, and marched ahead of him up the wooden stairs to the railed veranda which wrapped around three sides of the house.

She had to wait, straight-backed, as he sorted through the bunch of keys he had carried from the car, but before he inserted the correct one in the brass lock he answered one of her unspoken questions with a terse, 'I don't want my mother upset.'

'What?'

'My mother. Her health hasn't been the best since Zach's death. I don't want her involved in any of this. If you have anything to say, say it to me, not to her. Understand?'

She understood an order when she heard one. She reacted instinctively, bristling. She had lost one too many battles today to kowtow to someone who had no authority to make demands. She looked up at his grimly handsome face, thinking that it was too bad somebody had already broken his arrogant nose for him.

'Or...?'

His eyes darkened to pure gold menace. 'Or I'll make damned sure you regret it.'

Her thick dark brows lowered in what she liked to think was a threatening glower, the smattering of freckles on her smooth, winter-pale forehead jumping to attention as she rumpled it into soft pleats. 'You can try!'

He blinked at her pugnacious challenge, as if disconcerted by the novelty of opposition. Then he took a step closer, squaring his impressive shoulders, and Honor might have weakened and cringed but for the fact that the door suddenly whipped open between them.

'Adam, you're back! I thought I heard voices out here. And who's this you've brought to see me? Well,

well...come in, come in, don't stand out there, you might catch a chill...'

Still chattering delightedly, the elderly woman in oddly mismatched clothing drew Honor into the lighted hallway with a gnarled hand on her wrist, ignoring Adam's attempted explanation as he followed them inside.

'This is Honor Sheldon, Mother. She's going to stay with us for a few days——'

'How lovely to see you, my dear!' His mother overrode his curt statement with a gushing welcome. To Honor's bewilderment she was swept into a warm and surprisingly powerful hug from an old lady who was supposedly in frail health. She was tall and very thin, her white hair permed into a wild fluffiness that seemed to billow about her lined face as she beamed into her guest's confused eyes.

'I just *knew* that one of these days Adam was going to bring his girlfriend to see me,' she said gleefully, the fine network of lines on her face deepening with her smile as she barely paused for breath. 'He's been so elusive I knew he had to have someone very special tucked away and now here you are! You must be very good for him, Honor, because I can see he's looking very bright-eyed and bushy-tailed.' She cast her incredulous son a teasing look before her beaming brown eyes moved back to Honor's flushed face. 'And don't you two look good together—Adam so tall and husky and you so feminine— heart-high and lovely and curvy...'

It was certainly a very kindly and diplomatic way of calling someone short and fat, thought Honor wryly, knowing that her baggy jeans and faded shirt weren't very flattering, let alone feminine. She opened her mouth to correct Mrs Blake's disastrous first impression but Adam got there before her.

'She's not——'

'Now, Adam, don't try and pretend that this is just a casual visit,' his mother scolded him. 'You know you've never brought any of your lady-friends to stay before.

You can't tell me that Honor isn't different. Why, I can see she is. And she's blushing...'

'That's because you're embarrassing her——'

'Nonsense, dear! You're not embarrassed, are you, Honor?'

Shocked, confused, even amused—but no, Honor wasn't embarrassed. She was enjoying the sight of Adam's angry chagrin too much. Why should she help the surly brute out of the hole he had dug for himself?

'No, of course I'm not.'

'There! You see, Adam, the girl knows that she doesn't have to stand on ceremony with family.' She tilted her head confidingly towards Honor but made no attempt to lower her voice.

'My son is quite ridiculously protective, you know. He has this odd idea that I live in quite the past and don't know what sort of thing goes on in the modern world. But I know that young men and women have a great deal more freedom than they did in my day. Not that I approve of young people living together willy-nilly...'

'Honor and I are *not* living together——' Adam began firmly.

'You will be while you're both here, dear,' his mother pointed out with inescapable logic, and Honor almost giggled at the frustrated expression on Adam's face.

'We're just——' Adam faltered and looked at Honor, as if she might provide him with a suitably innocuous explanation of her presence.

She raised her eyebrows at him.

'Just good friends?' she suggested sweetly. To her gratification a flare of red appeared along the grim cheekbones.

'Of course you are, dear,' his mother soothed fondly, looking from one to the other with an expression of loving disbelief. Adam looked as if he was about to explode and Honor decided that the joke had gone far enough.

'Er—Mrs Blake——'

'Oh, call me Joy! I just know we're going to be won-derful friends. I've always got on very well with my sons' wives.'

'Mother!' Adam's protest was a muted roar. So much for his protective instincts!

'We're not getting married, Mrs—Joy——' interceded Honor hastily. 'I mean, we hardly know each other——'

Joy Blake seemed undismayed by the contradiction of her fantasies. She raised her hands protestingly and chuckled. 'I know, I know—it's too soon to trust your feelings. I know just what you're going through. I'm afraid the Blake men are prone to lightning attractions and whirlwind courtships. Adam's father and I met and married in two weeks when he was on furlough from the army. Well, once you settle in here and see how welcome you are I'm sure you'll be able to make up your mind about my son. He's a fine man, if a bit set in his ways. Goodness, dear, what is it you have in the box? Whatever it is, it sounds as if it's in great distress...'

Dazed by the speed and dexterity with which the elderly woman leapfrogged to ever more bizarre conclusions, Honor reacted too late. Joy Blake had the box out of her hand and on the floor and was opening it before she could get a protest out. Monty's flat, malevolent face appeared instantly, sniffing suspiciously at the strange environment before retreating as the rest of his body flattened, bunching for a spring.

'Why, it's a darling pussycat—aren't you a sweetie...?'

As Joy bent and reached eagerly into the box both Honor and Adam cried out simultaneous warnings:

'No, wait!'

'Don't touch that ani——!'

The protests died abruptly as Joy straightened up with Monty clasped to the dark red blouse that clashed so badly with her purple skirt.

'Oh, aren't you just adorable?' she cooed, pushing her face against his bristling fur.

Honor watched open-mouthed as her irascible pet went limp and allowed himself to be nuzzled and chucked under the chin by a total stranger. Even more staggering, he actually began his motoring purr and aimed a few swipes of his raspy tongue at Joy's stroking fingers. Out of the corner of her eye Honor could see Adam wearing a stunned look very similar to her own.

Joy laughed. 'What's your name, cutie?'

Cutie? Honor had heard Monty called plenty of names—including a few imaginative ones coined by Adam tonight—but never had anyone suggested that *cuteness* was one of his feline attributes.

'He's called Monty,' she said faintly, wondering if the trauma of travel had temporarily altered his personality for the better.

'I bet you're hungry, aren't you, fella? Why don't I take him into the kitchen while you two go upstairs and change for dinner? It'll be ready in about half an hour.'

'I've already eaten,' Honor said hastily.

'Oh, that's a shame.' Joy Blake shook her head. 'I've invented this lovely Mediterranean chicken casserole dish and I would have appreciated another opinion. I've used dried fruits and almonds and cinnamon and ginger...' She smiled coaxingly at Honor. 'Are you sure you couldn't manage even a nibble?'

Honor's stomach was remembering the chocolate-cake bribe that hadn't quite compensated for the wizened omelette. Her taste-buds moistened. 'Well, maybe a little——'

'I thought we'd agreed that you were supposed to be taking things easy,' Adam interrupted, frowning at his mother. 'You don't have to bother with the cooking. That's what Rhonda's employed for——'

'It so happens, Adam, that I *like* to bother with the cooking,' his mother told him, her smile fading as she faced him, still hugging the purring cat to her chest. 'And you needn't worry. I didn't do anything more taxing than stir a few pots. Rhonda did all the carrying and chopping and running around. I just sat back and gave her instructions.'

As Adam continued to regard her with a worried expression Joy Blake's confidence visibly wavered and she stroked Monty's fur with a finely trembling hand, her faded brown eyes clouding over. She pinned a determined, if slightly shaky smile back on her face as she turned towards Honor, immediately launching forth into the breathless chatter with which she had first greeted them.

'Now, don't you fret about Monty; we're friends already and once I feed him he'll settle in nicely. We have a cat ourselves so there's plenty of cat food in the kitchen and I'll make a place for him to sleep unless you want to have him in your room.

'And talking of rooms, Adam...' she turned back to her son, lifting her chin haughtily '... I'll leave you to decide where to put Honor. I don't want to be accused of being a nosy, interfering old woman so I'll just say whatever sleeping arrangements you choose to make will be fine by me. Although you might want to bear in mind that certain others who live here might not be as accommodating!'

And with that obscurely pointed jab she retreated down the hall, Monty's tail waving like a victory flag behind her back, vanishing through a wooden swing door at the far end, giving Honor a brief glimpse of the large, brightly lit, tiled kitchen beyond.

Honor was still wearing an involuntary smile when she turned back to Adam. 'Is she always like that?'

'Like what?'

He looked so ready to bite her head off that Honor decided she would be unwise to say that she found his mother very entertaining. He was bound to take it the wrong way.

'So... welcoming.'

He glared, as if he knew that she had mentally edited her reply. Just to needle him, she added, 'She seemed to think that we're heavily involved with each other.'

'I wonder where she got that impression?' he snarled sarcastically. 'What the hell did you have to mouth that cliché about being "just good friends" for? You must have known the interpretation she'd put on it.'

'Well, what did you expect me to say when you just stood there stammering like an idiot?' she demanded. 'If you knew you were going to have to lie you might have at least had the sense to cook up a good one before we got here. I was just trying to help you out.'

'The hell you were! You said it purely to make trouble. I *was* going to tell her that you were a new secretary here to do some work for me——'

'You could still tell her that,' Honor said, feeling guilty at the truth of his accusation. At the time she hadn't been concerned with anything but petty point-scoring.

'She knows I don't play around with my secretaries,' he gritted.

'Uh—I'm glad to hear it,' said Honor in a weak attempt to lighten the atmosphere.

'And certainly no secretary of mine would bring a damned cat to work with her!'

Honor's eyes narrowed. Even guilt had its limits. 'You can't blame that on me. I didn't want to come here in the first place. And your mother seemed awfully anxious to whip up a passionate affair out of nothing. I wonder why that is?'

He ignored her, picking up the suitcase that he had hastily dropped in anticipation of having to rescue his mother from Monty's temper and indicating the stairs to their left with a sharp inclination of his blond head. The overhead light revealed reddish glints hidden among the gold. An incipient redhead. No wonder he had a healthy temper, Honor thought as she followed him silently up the wide wooden staircase. Actually, he could do with a haircut. The lighter blond ends which brushed the crew neck of his sweater were uneven, frosted and split by exposure to the sun. She also noticed that although the black trousers and sweater sported expensive designer motifs the sweater was worn thin on one elbow and the trousers had a frayed back pocket. Obviously not a man who put a lot of emphasis on sartorial elegance. Maybe he didn't worry about dressing to impress because he knew he was all too impressive whatever he wore. Her eyes fell further and widened. He was wearing odd socks: one dark grey, one black. She grinned, irrationally reassured by the absent-minded chink in his forcefully confident appearance.

'You find my home amusing?'

She reached the top of the stairs to find Adam staring at her curving mouth with a mixture of belligerence and suspicion.

'*Your* home?' She was disconcerted. 'I thought you lived on the North Shore?'

'I inherited this place from Zach.'

So his brother had had no wife or children of his own... 'Are you going to be living here from now on?'

His eyes narrowed. 'Why do you want to know?'

She squinted back. 'I thought I might semaphore the information out the window to my criminal cohorts atop the next ridge.'

For a moment she thought she saw a quiver of amusement touch the hard mouth but his reply was hopelessly pedantic.

'You know semaphore?'

'I was a crack Guide,' she lied. 'I try always to be prepared.'

'I thought that was the Scout motto,' he said drily.

She looked at him in mock-dismay. 'No wonder there was always a rush to share my tent when we went camping!'

Definitely a grin, but he turned away before she could fully appreciate its effect on his tanned features and strode along the hall to push open one of the pale doors.

The room was large and uncluttered, the painted cream walls and warm apricot accents in the draperies a clever contrast to the cool blues and greys that predominated in what she had so far seen of the rest of the place. A single bed covered with a billowing quilt inhabited the far corner and adjacent to it was a broad sash window which overlooked the rear of the property.

'What, no bars?' murmured Honor tartly, to hide the unexpected sense of welcome the room gave her. She crossed to peer out of the window, noting the irregularly shaped swimming-pool which glittered darkly in the dimly lit fenced gardens below.

'I'm sure I can arrange to have some installed if that'll make you feel safer, Honor.'

She spun around at the bland comment. Now the glint of humour in the brown eyes was unconcealed and Honor was perversely annoyed by his amusement. 'That's not what I meant——'

'Then what *did* you mean? You're a guest here, not a prisoner. See, your door doesn't even have a lock on it.' He swung it on its hinges to show her both sides.

'And *that's* supposed to reassure me?' Honor goaded with heavy sarcasm. 'Your hospitality must be really dire if you have to resort to threatening people to get them to come and stay. If I really am a guest then I guess Monty and I are free to leave when we like...?'

'Of course,' he agreed, adding smoothly, 'Ignoring police advice may be foolish and in this case probably quite dangerous, but it's certainly not illegal...'

She gave him a fulminating look that had no effect whatsoever on his smug confidence. If she had known how aggravating he was in person she would never have fallen in love with his letters.

'What's in here? The bathroom?' She flung open the door next to the wardrobe, resorting to action to divert her dangerous thoughts.

'No, I'm afraid you have to share the bathroom,' he said with suspicious meekness. 'It's two doors down the hall on the right.'

She was staring at the room which interconnected with hers, an intensely masculine room with a huge brass bedstead that dominated everything else.

'This is your room,' she guessed accusingly, letting go the door-handle as if it were a red-hot coal. 'Why am I in the room next to yours?'

'Because it's the only one available.'

She would have liked to call him a liar but since there was a slight chance he might be telling the truth she kept her mouth shut. She had made enough of a fool of herself in front of him for one day.

'I suppose there's no key to *this* door, either?' she snapped, closing it again with exaggerated care, shutting out the view of that looming, masculine bed.

He shrugged. 'What can I say?' He spread his big hands palm up in a gesture of mock-helplessness. 'We're a very trusting family.'

Oh, yes, his mood had turned very affable now he was getting his own way.

'Well, I'm not one of the family and I don't trust you,' she told him grittily.

'The feeling is entirely mutual,' he assured her.

'I'm scarcely likely to sneak into your room and try and overpower *you*,' she pointed out.

He raised his eyebrows. 'It sounds like wish transference to me. Is that what you're hoping I might do? Don't let your frustrated-spinster fantasies run away with you, Honor. They've got you into enough trouble as it is——'

'*My* fantasies?' Her temper hotted up again. 'You're a fine one to criticise. You——'

'Let's not get into another round of pointless argument,' he cut her off succinctly. 'Suffice it to say that I've never been so hard up for sex that I had to resort to violence to get it.'

She believed him. With his looks and his wealth he would have no trouble attracting women. She found it hard to superimpose that confident image on the man of letters who had so enchanted her with his sensitivity. If it hadn't been shyness or social awkwardness that had prompted him to hide behind a box number, had it merely been an experiment, an idle mental exercise in seduction without the complications of a fully fledged affair? A new fillip for a jaded male palate? But then the last few frantic letters made nonsense of that theory. They had been nothing short of a raw demand for a physical consummation of their relationship. Not even an invitation—a *demand* ...

'Neither have I,' she said bluntly, trying for the same blend of arrogance and sexual sophistication he was displaying. She wasn't going to let him intimidate her into feeling inferior. She let her eyes drift over him with what she hoped was a suitably haughty disdain.

'Good, then neither of us has to lie awake tonight worrying whether we're about to be ravished in our bed.'

The notion of her small body physically overpowering his huge, solid frame was ludicrous. As for forcing him to make love to her, Honor didn't think such a thing could physically be accomplished...unless—— Her eyes flicked to the adjoining door and a vivid mental picture arose in her head. Unless she crept in and tied him to the convenient bars of his brass bedstead while he was still asleep and then, when he was utterly at her mercy...

Honor closed her eyes, blushing hotly as she realised where her thoughts were taking her. She was shocked at herself. Did his taunt have some basis after all? Was she becoming obsessed with unhealthy fantasies at the expense of drab reality? Reality being that if it were *Helen* whom Adam had dragged up here he wouldn't be rejecting the possibility of ravishment!

'Don't flatter yourself!' she managed weakly, at last, opening her eyes to deny the power of the wicked images behind her closed lids. To her horror he was studying her guilty blush with mocking speculation.

'Was I? No need to get flustered, Miss Sheldon, your naughty secrets are safe with me...*I'm* not in the trade of buying and selling private conversations.'

The slightly grim edge to his mockery had Honor floundering for a fittingly acid reply as he continued coolly, 'May I suggest you take my mother's advice and change before you go down for dinner? We don't bother with formality but we do expect guests to be clean and reasonably dressed. In that tatty ensemble you'll probably shed cat fur all over the table.'

With that masterly final insult he vanished into his bedroom, shutting the connecting door with a quiet click that punctuated Honor's open-mouthed silence.

'Well, of all the...!'

She wished she had a stunning cocktail dress she could whip out of her suitcase and use to knock his arrogant eyes out.

Alas, she discovered as she ferreted through the clothes that Adam had carelessly stuffed into her suitcase, nothing he had brought matched. He had included the bottom half of two suits and the top half of a third, a skirt and blouse that didn't match, a dress that she hadn't worn for at least three years and another that she didn't even remember possessing, and assorted bits and bobs that didn't go with anything else.

First things first. She nipped along to the big, old-fashioned but very functional bathroom and washed her face and hands. When she came back she wedged the bedroom chair under the handle of the connecting door and peeled off her clothes.

The black dress that she didn't remember seemed her best bet but when she struggled into it she realised why it had seemed so unfamiliar. It was one of Helen's discards, several of which hung, largely unworn, in the back of Honor's wardrobe. What looked elegant on Helen's willowy size ten verged on the tacky when draped on a figure which hovered erratically between size twelve and fourteen, even though the famous designer label claimed the figure-hugging tube was of the 'one size fits all' variety.

It had undoubtedly been a mini on Helen, revealing a startling amount of long, slender leg. On Honor the length was more modest but the fit definitely wasn't. It was desperately tight cross the hips and bust and although the stretchy, bubble-knit fabric hid a multitude of sins there was no getting away from the fact that it made her look disappointingly lumpy. Her bra straps refused to align with the cut-away shoulders, further destroying the elegant simplicity of line, although at least the front was high enough to hide the thin scratches that marred her chest. She muttered darkly to herself, cursing high-fashion designers who refused to acknowledge that most of the world's women didn't conform to their artificial standards of bodily perfection.

She rifled back through her suitcase and came up with a short-cropped red cardigan. A jacket would have been better but this would have to do. She pulled it on. It created a much less tarty effect. She couldn't wear stockings because she didn't have a suitable slip to stop them sticking to the knit skirt but thankfully her legs were evenly tanned from her gardening and at least Adam had, obviously by mistake, included some flatteringly high-heeled black shoes that would minimise the flare of her calves. She dragged a brush ruthlessly through her hair, grimacing at the knots and the way it sprang up again in a crackling frenzy. The harder she tried to control it, the more it disobeyed.

The carpet on the floor was thick and the house seemed strangely hushed as she found her way back downstairs. Always sensitive to atmosphere, Honor felt a prickling unease as she moved along the ground-floor hall, passing several fastidiously neat rooms furnished in a jarring mixture of the starkly modern and comfortably antique. The silence was almost unnatural, as if the house were watching her progress disapprovingly, isolating her within its walls, waiting for her to set the first foot wrong.

A whisper of sound had her quickening her step to push open the double doors opposite the kitchen, grateful that she'd found the dining-room at last.

Expecting to see only Adam and his mother, she was startled to find two other people with them. One was a slender, strikingly attractive brunette in her mid-thirties and the other was a plump, blonde-haired child of about ten or eleven whose mouth fell rudely open as Joy Blake hustled forward.

'Honor, come in, don't be shy—come in and meet my daughter-in-law, Tania. She's just arrived with Adam's daughter, Sara. Sara, say hello to Miss Sheldon...'

A loud buzzing invaded Honor's skull. Adam was *married*? Adam was married to this glamorous woman! And he had a *daughter*...a girl who, by the way she was clinging tightly to her father's hand, adored him.

The swine! The lying, hypocritical, faithless *devil*! No wonder he had been so frantic to get those compromising letters back!

Honor marched into the room giving him a searing look that she was pleased to see wiped the tentative half-smile off his face to be replaced with a tiny, nervous, downward twitch. Good, he was worried. He deserved to be! She had the ammunition to blow this little game of happy families wide apart!

CHAPTER FIVE

THE dinner was every bit as delicious as Joy Blake had promised it would be, but in spite of her best intentions Honor had difficulty enjoying a single bite.

For one thing Adam's weird daughter watched her like a hawk from across the table, following the progress of every mouthful with a kind of horrified fascination, as if expecting at any moment that Honor was going to transmogrify from an ordinary woman into a hideous monster.

Every time Honor tried to address a friendly remark to her, the dark brown gaze would skitter away and the girl would give a very good impression of being both deaf and dumb. Honor didn't have a lot of experience with children, but Adam had mentioned that Sara was twelve and Honor thought that was plenty old enough to have acquired a *few* social graces.

The blatantly hostile vibes emanating from the foot of the table were another keen appetite-suppressant.

Under her cold and haughty exterior Tania Blake was seething with tension. Honor had recognised the type on sight—her sister's milieu was crowded with them—women dedicated to the pursuit of personal ambition, social piranhas who cruised conversations in search of a kill that would enhance their own standing. Their lethal use of witticism and innuendo to vanquish rivals had always reminded her of an eighteenth-century poet's cynical reference to society gossip: 'At ev'ry word a reputation dies.'

Eyeing the electric-blue Thai silk dress and heavy gold jewellery that created such a vibrant impression in the serene dining-room, Honor felt miserably at a disadvantage, physical as well as psychological. Her anger at

Adam re-ignited, burning away her embarrassment at the invidious position in which his flagrant literary—if not literal—unfaithfulness had placed her. If Tania was a piranha then Adam had exactly the kind of wife he deserved!

Unfortunately Honor's haste to dissociate herself with his perfidity only plunged her into deeper embarrassment.

If only she had waited for Joy to finish her rambling introduction instead of rushing into speech, but when the beautiful woman at Adam's side had greeted her with icy distaste Honor had felt compelled to try and explain.

'Mrs Blake——' there had been no friendly 'call me Tania' and, from the looks of things, was not likely to be! '—I *assure* you that I wouldn't have invaded your home like this if...if the police hadn't *insisted*——'

To her horror Adam interrupted curtly.

'You mean if *I* hadn't insisted. There's no need to make excuses for me, Honor. I didn't ask for your protection and I don't need it.'

Honor turned on him fiercely, holding her head so that her mouth couldn't be seen by his family as she whispered fiercely at him in an undertone, 'No, but your wife and child might!'

Adam didn't even have the decency to look ashamed. 'My wife?'

'My God, you really don't have a single shred of conscience, do you?'

'*Honor*——'

'You faithless pig, don't you Honor *me*——!'

To her intense fury his despicably attractive mouth quirked, as if he suddenly found the horrible situation amusing. 'All right, I won't honour you, but don't blame me if you don't like the consequences.'

Her chest puffed up in rage, an effect that he then had the gall to study openly. It was very difficult to cut a man down with a glare when all his attention was fixed on her breasts. No doubt he thought them too large.

Helen had actually suggested a breast-reduction operation, but then Helen considered anything larger than
thirty-four A to be grossly inflated! Suddenly realising
where her thoughts were leading—as if she *cared* what
a married man thought of her breasts—Honor whipped
herself up to fresh fury.

She wished there were some physical flaw of his that
she could stare rudely at, but unfortunately even the
slight crookedness of his nose was singularly attractive
and the rest of his body was shrouded in a sports jacket
and trousers of casual but impeccable cut. She checked
his feet. To her frustration his socks matched and his
dark shoes gleamed. Her chin went up as she resorted
to verbal insult to cut him down to size.

'How dare you treat your wife with so little consideration? Have you no shame, you...you *roué*?'

It was an absurdly old-fashioned word, but one that
fitted him perfectly. Unfortunately she had forgotten to
keep her voice down.

'Wife?' Tania caught his arm, her voice rising from
cultured haughtiness to a strident shrill, her blue eyes
glittering with distaste. 'My God, Adam, you haven't
gone and got yourself *married* to this...this *person*?'

Honor blanched. If Tania thought he was married to
Honor, then that must mean...

'Don't be ridiculous, Tania,' said Adam, shaking off
her clutching hand. 'Do you really think I'd get married
again without asking Sara's permission?' He looked
down at his daughter's anxiously upturned face and his
voice softened. 'You know I wouldn't do that, don't you,
honey?'

His daughter nodded jerkily, her glance swivelling back
in wide-eyed curiosity to Honor.

'Well, what did she say about a wife, then?' Tania
said sharply, her manicured fingers curling into his sleeve
again. '*Something* is going on and I demand to
know what it is!'

'You can *ask* all you want, but you won't necessarily get a reply. As Zachary's widow you deserve respect and consideration, not chapter and verse on my business and private affairs.'

Adam plucked her fingers from his arm for a second time as he pointedly emphasised their relationship, not taking his eyes off Honor's face as she realised what he was telling her.

Her complexion went from pale anger to fiery embarrassment in the space of a single heartbeat. Tania was his *sister-in-law*. Oh, *no*!

'Perhaps you'd care to rephrase some of your remarks now, Honor?' said Adam silkily, enjoying her obvious mortification so much that her pride rebelled against the necessity of apologising.

'I...it was a natural mistake to make in the circumstances,' she mumbled defensively.

Tania didn't give the impression of being a grieving widow. Not that Honor would expect her still to be wearing black or walking around with red-rimmed eyes months after her husband's death, but feminine intuition told her that that electric-blue dress was designed—and worn—to achieve maximum male impact. And the only male around here within impacting distance was Adam.

'Was it?' He was unrelenting. Hadn't she faced enough tough questions and moral dilemmas already today?

'Well, I...you...'

He nodded and said sardonically, 'I'm a roué, a conscienceless bully and a kidnapper...so it follows therefore that I'm also completely amoral.'

'Kidnapper?' Tania's beautiful face hardened with frustrated curiosity at the increasingly cryptic nature of the conversation. 'Whom have you kidnapped? What's going on?'

'Where did you get that scratch on your face, Daddy?'

The Adam who so effortlessly ignored his beautiful sister-in-law gave instant attention to his daughter.

'A wildcat got me,' he smiled, touching the dark golden strands which almost hid the mark on his forehead. Even Honor, who knew it was there, had to look for it. His daughter was obviously extremely observant.

'A wildcat!' Sara's freckled forehead wrinkled. 'You mean, like a tiger or something?'

'Well, not quite that kind of a wildcat,' her father told her. He turned his amused gaze to Honor who unaccountably blushed. Joy looked amused, too, while Tania's mouth twisted with haughty distaste. Oh, no, surely they didn't think that *she* ...?

Adam put his arm around Sara, pulling her close into his side. Two sets of brown eyes regarded Honor's vivid embarrassment. Two against one. 'Why don't we ask our guest to explain? She works for the local free newspaper. Words are her stock-in-trade.'

God, he was really determined to rub it in!

'A journalist,' Tania burst out stridently. 'I thought you told me you didn't want anyone from the Press here. Even if she only works for a hick weekly she's still a reporter——'

'Bi-weekly, actually,' Adam interrupted pedantically, 'but as it happens Honor isn't here in a professional capacity and she would never dream of betraying the confidence of a friend for the sake of a quick buck, would you, sweetheart?'

Sweetheart?

The steely-tender endearment was as loaded a threat as she had ever heard. Honor gulped and summoned a weak smile.

'Er—yes—I mean, no...' Even to her own ears she sounded disgustingly feeble. She drew herself up and glared at Adam. 'Not unless the *friend* had proved to be unworthy of the name. After all, trust works both ways, doesn't it ... *darling*?'

She was sorry that she had used the taunting appellation when she saw Sara Blake bite her lip hard and look down at her feet, her hand tightening on her father's.

In her pin-tucked white blouse and tartan pleated skirt the girl suddenly looked younger than her years. It wasn't fair that she should be made to suffer for Adam's infuriating behaviour. Honor looked away, right into the spotlight of Tania's hostile stare, and felt even more guilty. In the circumstances the family had every right to fear Press involvement.

Everyone except Joy, it seemed, who alleviated the suddenly sizzling silence by clapping her hands. 'So you're a writer, how delightful! Do you know, Adam used to be a bit of a wordsmith himself when he was younger? He always used to get top marks for his essays at school. He had such a marvellous imagination...' She sighed. 'I thought that he might be a famous author one day...'

'Don't be ridiculous, Joy.' Tania gave a dismissive little laugh. 'Adam's always been a man of action. He wouldn't be satisfied sitting down at a desk scribbling all day. He likes being in the thick of the action. That's why the farm couldn't hold him—it wasn't enough of a challenge. He had to go out and create his own.'

Joy Blake subsided like a pricked balloon and Honor felt a surge of sympathy. Her involvement with old people through the Talking Books scheme had taught her that of all the sins committed against the aged the most frequent and most damaging to their pride was the casual impatience with which their views and opinions were often brushed aside.

'Adam's imagination's been put to far better use than it would have been as a mere purveyor of information to the masses,' Tania continued to press her point in the same condescending tone. 'If it weren't for his ideas and urging, Zach never would have embarked on a diversification programme and the Blake companies wouldn't be as profitable as they are today. Adam has achieved the kind of success that most people only dream of.' The condescension deepened as Tania turned her critical attention back to Honor, her smile anything but kind. 'Judging from the outfit Miss Sheldon's wearing, I don't suppose that writing is a very lucrative career...'

Ouch! Honor's estimation of the woman went down another notch.

'Actually this dress is a Paris original,' she drawled with a fairly good imitation of Tania's own haughty speech, and name-dropped the prestigious French designer that Helen had been wild about a few years ago when she had bought the dress. No need to mention that the cardigan was from the bargain-bin of a chain store!

Unfortunately her remark had the effect of drawing all eyes to her rounded figure and she stiffened uncomfortably, resisting the urge to pull the edges of the cardigan across her breasts like a self-conscious adolescent ill at ease with her body. But that was how she felt. Adam's eyes were gleaming with a faintly lecherous malice as they drifted down past her hips and crawled slowly back up to her breasts. Her fingers twitched with the effort of restraint. He was doing it deliberately, damn it, and if he kept it up she was going to slap his face and to hell with what his family thought!

As if he knew what was going through her mind he stepped back out of range and politely suggested it was time they sat down, shepherding them all to their seats at the table. His harem, thought Honor darkly as dinner was served by yet another female—a cheerful, middle-aged woman whom Adam addressed as Rhonda. After transferring the dishes from the trolley to the table, Rhonda said goodnight and withdrew with a frankly curious glance at Honor, whom Adam had insisted on seating beside him.

Honor had expected that Joy would ease the tension over dinner with more of her delightfully artless chatter, but the older woman was subdued as her daughter-in-law effortlessly dominated the conversation. In very short order she chiselled out of Honor where she lived, whom she worked for and how old she was. When Honor fended off other enquiries with polite generalities, furious with Adam for abandoning her to the intrusive questioning, Tania talked about herself, painting a picture of domestic contentment that Honor found difficult to believe, given the woman's air of restless discontent.

As she doggedly moved the chicken from side to side on her plate, Honor listened to how Tania had spent the last few days staying at Adam's North Shore home while she shopped and attended several social events in the city.

'Did the sales finish early, or are you off back to town again tomorrow?' Adam finally put in drily. 'We didn't expect you back until the weekend.'

'Perhaps I missed your scintillating company,' Tania laughed back, not at all put out by his cynical implication. 'Since I had to drop Sara off I decided it was silly to turn around and go all that way back for just another day or two. You know I love your house but it's very lonely rattling around there by myself. I much prefer it when you're there to keep me company.'

Honor didn't need to be told that she was the target of the coyly pouting remark, rather than the man at whom it was ostensibly aimed.

'Do you know Adam's house?' Tania's eyes were cool with not-so-innocent enquiry. 'Did he tell you he designed it himself? It really surprised everyone. Those sinful bathrooms. Why, you could get lost in them for a week!'

Having established her intimate familiarity with Adam's life, Tania allowed herself a smug pause.

Honor was being warned off. It should have been amusing but for some reason it stung.

'I wasn't in the least surprised,' she purred, casting Adam a melting look that halted him in mid-chew. He had described some of his home's peculiarities in one of his letters. 'I always knew that Adam was a man with hidden depths. I think his house is a reflection of his character—full of imaginative angles and impulsive fantasies.'

'Adam is the least impulsive man I know,' Tania corrected testily.

'As I said, a man with hidden depths,' Honor murmured with a shrug that was intended to annoy. She lowered her normally husky voice even further. 'You and I obviously see very different sides to him.'

'You obviously don't know him as well as you think you do.' Politeness no longer sheathed Tania's curiosity. Her suspicion broke cover into open interrogation. 'If this is the first time you've met Sara then you and Adam can't have been seeing each other for very long, because we all know how he likes to show her off. Just when *did* you and Adam meet each other?'

Honor's mouth was open to fend off the query when she felt a large warm hand close firmly on her knee.

'It seems like aeons ago but it was actually only a few months,' Adam interposed smoothly with the literal truth. 'I'm afraid I've been totally selfish in wanting to keep Honor to myself, but thanks to Sara's unexpected lapse in conduct I've now rectified the omission.' He turned to address his wary daughter. 'On which subject I'll only say I find it very strange that a straight-A student who has always been praised for her mature attitudes should suddenly be sent home in disgrace. You *begged* me to let you stay at the same school while we were living here, even though it meant making special travel arrangements for the extra distance. I hope this incident doesn't indicate that I made a bad mistake...'

Honor realised that the tension she had encountered in the dining-room hadn't been purely a result of her own arrival. It was something of a relief to find someone else on the receiving end of Adam's disapprobation.

'You've been expelled?' Honor couldn't help exclaiming. Adam had revealed himself to be so erudite in his letters that she was surprised he hadn't instilled the same respect for learning in his offspring. The restraining hand slid away from her knee, leaving her with an unexpected feeling of abandonment.

'Suspended,' the girl corrected, shooting an uneasy look at her father's thoughtful face.

'Wow...what did you do?' In spite of her best attempt to hide it, Honor heard a sly trace of admiration leak into her voice. Having been a 'goody-goody' all through school, victim of her respect for authority and fear of getting caught, she had always had a sneaking envy for those reckless souls who had flouted the rules.

The girl evidently heard it, too, because suddenly the brown eyes fixed directly on Honor's for the first time. 'I was caught with a packet of cigarettes.'

'On three separate occasions in one week,' added her father evenly, stressing the ongoing nature of her offending.

'Help!' Glad that the crime was of a relatively minor nature, although she hoped the girl was experimenting rather than seriously smoking, Honor composed her expression into what she thought was a suitably shocked look. It evidently didn't quite make the grade because it brought forth a cheeky grin from the miscreant.

'That's what Miss Runcie said I needed. She said I should visit the medical school and have a look at the cancer-riddled lungs they have in jars. Gross! I don't know what she was so het up about. I only managed a few puffs before I was caught.'

Three times in a week? Once was understandable. Twice was foolish. Three times smacked of either arrant stupidity or a plea for attention. No wonder Adam was puzzled.

'That isn't quite the point, Sara,' Tania interceded, adopting a sternly lecturing tone. 'You know very well why the headmistress was het up. You were warned of the consequences of you breaking the rules again and yet you still went ahead and did it. You not only let yourself down, you let your father and me down, too. Imagine how shocked and humiliated I felt, as a former head girl of the school, to be rung up and told of your disgraceful conduct——'

'She didn't ring you, she rang Dad,' Sara pointed out. 'She was just so mad she'd forgotten that he had moved over here.'

'*She* is the cat's mother, Sara,' said Tania, using the prim cliché that had always infuriated a youthful Honor when adults had used it as a grammatical reproof. Sure enough, Sara rolled her eyes in the silent equivalent of a disgusted snort.

'Mistake or not, she spoke to me first,' Tania continued in the same patronising vein. 'And since your father wasn't available I exercised my responsibility as your closest adult female relative.' Nobody remarked on Tania's overlooking of Joy's greater claim to a blood-tie as she steamed ahead. 'In fact it was only due to my influence with Miss Runcie that you weren't expelled outright. And you haven't even bothered to thank me for my intervention.'

Sara shrugged. 'Thanks, *Aunt* Tania.' The emphasis was just subtle enough to pass unnoticed, except to Honor who was beginning to realise that this family was anything but straightforward.

Sara's attitude didn't seem like the sullen defiance of a hardened delinquent. Honor had seen a few of those at the American high school from which she had graduated. Alcohol and hard drugs had featured prominently in their protests which were invariably self-destructive. Sara, in contrast, seemed to have the serenely martyred air of someone enduring a temporary trial for the sake of the greater good of mankind.

'Yes, thanks, Tania,' Adam said, with a similar lack of enthusiasm. 'I'm sorry you were bothered with our problems——'

'It wasn't a bother at all. Who can you rely on to help you if not your family?' said Tania, giving him a brilliant smile that he deflected with a wry one of his own. 'I was just surprised that no one seemed to know where you were. When I asked Joy she didn't seem to know...'

'But you didn't tell me what you wanted him for,' Joy began with a frown. 'If you'd told me it was urgent I would have tried to find him.'

Tania looked at her. 'But I did tell you, don't you remember?' The old woman hesitated and Tania smiled at her soothingly. 'Don't worry, Joy, we understand... your memory isn't what it was when you were younger. You panicked when I mentioned Sara and probably just got confused. Never mind. No harm done... this time.'

Except to Joy's confidence. Honor noticed the fleeting fear that invaded the faded brown eyes and the way the elderly hands tightened on her knife and fork. Couldn't Tania see that her reassurances were having the opposite effect?

'I've got a memory like a sieve, myself,' Honor said, smiling cheerfully at Joy. 'Especially for names. This chicken recipe of yours is really delicious by the way, Joy; you must write it down for me because I'm hopeless at remembering lists of ingredients. That's why I became a reporter—I was always having to write things down to remember them, so I figured why not make a profession of it? It used to drive my sister crazy when I mixed up her phone messages, especially when she'd go out to meet someone for a date and it would turn out to be with someone completely different—usually some nerd she'd been trying to fob off...'

'You have a sister? Older or younger?' Joy grasped gratefully at the change of topic and too late Honor realised she should have used a different example. For a blessed moment she had forgotten her own problems.

'Er—older; she lives in Manhattan.'

'New York?' Tania looked interested at the mention of the Big Apple. 'What does she do?'

'Helen's a model,' admitted Honor reluctantly.

'A very beautiful, blonde model.' Adam modified her bald statement in a way that set her teeth on edge.

'Helen Sheldon... *Helen Sheldon* is *your* sister?' asked Tania sharply. Honor sighed; she might have known that someone as exquisitely dressed as Tania would make the connection.

'Yes.'

'Goodness, I would never have guessed,' Tania drawled with a malicious chuckle. Honor had heard the comment so often that it was water off a duck's back. She merely smiled politely and Tania's eyes glittered with speculation as she positioned her next thrust. 'Is the dress one of hers? Is that why it looks so... unfamiliar on you?'

Great. Now everyone knew she was wearing a hand-me-down albeit an exclusive one. Honor decided there was little point in trying to preserve any of her sartorial pride.

'Whenever she visits she gives me her cast-offs.' She looked down at herself ruefully. 'Unfortunately she and I aren't exactly the same size... For one thing she's five feet eleven and thin as a rake... a natural blonde, too. I'm afraid that I must have got my parents' genetic left-overs.' She grinned at Sara. 'You ever see that Arnold Schwarzenegger-Danny De Vito movie *Twins*? That's Helen and me... needless to say I play the De Vito part!'

Instead of laughing Sara looked slightly green.

'Are you all right, honey?' asked her grandmother.

'Uh—yeah... excuse me, I just have to go to the—uh—I'll be back in a moment.' She rushed out of the room, all flying elbows and knees.

'Probably all that smoking playing havoc with her digestive system,' commented Tania sarcastically. 'You really should let me enrol her in a grooming course, Adam. It would give her so much more confidence. Then she wouldn't have to do stupid things to make herself popular with the other girls.'

'Is that why you think she did it?' Adam asked mildly.

Tania shrugged. 'Isn't peer pressure the usual reason for these things? Maybe if she could lose some of that pudge and acquire some clothes-sense she'd feel better about herself.'

'It's only puppy-fat, Tania,' Joy interceded. 'Remember, Mary was tall and slim so I'm sure Sara's body will mature into a very nice figure...' Her brow wrinkled anxiously. 'You don't really think she worries about it, do you, Adam? She's never said anything to me.'

'No offence, Joy, but Sara probably feels you're a bit out of touch with modern trends,' Tania said. 'It's been five years since her mother died; maybe she needs to unburden herself to a woman who is around the age Mary would have been ... Perhaps I could have a word with her, Adam, coax her to talk...'

'Or perhaps Honor could,' said Joy flatly.

Tania's eyes narrowed. 'Well, yes,' she said sweetly. 'I suppose it might help to talk with someone who has the same problems. But don't you think that Honor would be the wrong person to talk about shedding puppy-fat as one gets older? I mean, no offence, Honor, but you're not exactly role-model material in that respect.'

No offence? Distracted from her pondering on the subject of Adam's newly revealed widowhood, Honor boiled at the hypocrisy of the glib catch-phrase that Tania had used twice in as many minutes. She now went on to hammer her point home. 'You're also a living contradiction that likenesses necessarily run in families. Your sister would be a far better role-model for Sara to emulate. Have you met Honor's family, Adam? Do you know Helen?'

The hunt for information was back on. Honor turned her head to watch Adam take a sip of the white wine that he had opened with the meal. He had been behaving with strange passivity for such a dominating man, she suddenly realised. And it wasn't abstraction—his attention had been very much focused on the conversation across the dinner table. It was more likely he had been playing some kind of waiting game...watching, brooding, *planning*...

Honor took a nervous gulp from her own glass. She should never have provoked him earlier. What was he going to say now? Something provocative and clever like, I thought I did...? Yes, he'd probably love to make Honor squirm by saying something like that.

'We've met.'

Honor choked in mid-swallow at his succinct, unrevealing reply. Adam leaned over and gave her a sharp slap between the shoulderblades, taking the glass from her hand and setting it down on the table.

'All right, sweetheart?' he asked, his tender tone an unnerving contrast to the firmness of the blow.

'Yes, fine,' Honor coughed, wondering what he was up to now.

He leaned closer, cupping her chin and turning her head so that he could look deep into her watering eyes. 'You're sure?'

'Y-yes, yes, of course I'm sure. It just went down the wrong way,' she stammered, feeling vulnerable to the invisible daggers she was sure were thudding into her back. It didn't take much brain-power to work out that Tania had *very* possessive feelings about her brother-in-law.

A big hand tucked an errant curl behind her ear. 'Maybe you should go easy on the wine; it seems to have a very deleterious effect on your co-ordination,' he teased softly, in a voice that rasped Honor's nerves like a sand-paper caress. 'Remember the last party we attended together? You fell asleep and I had to carry you out to the car...'

His sensual innuendo was so disconcerting that it took a moment for her to recognise how cleverly he had mixed fact with fiction. He was talking about the night of the Valentine's Ball. The last party they had both attended? It was the *only* one! But he made the bare facts sound so *intimate*...

'That wasn't the wine, that was the medication I was taking,' she said, trying not to quiver at the stroke of his thumb along her captured jaw. Maybe if she could get in a little further explanation here, it would take the edge off whatever devil was driving him to play this alarming new game. 'I was sick that night, but I had to go to the ball because I was one of the organisers——'

His thumb shifted to press over her mouth, stopping her words. His hypnotic golden-brown eyes moved even closer, blocking out her awareness of anyone else at the table.

'Poor little Cinders. How lucky you had a prince to come to your rescue. Though I must admit, after what your sister told me, I half expected some jealous swain to swoop down on me and snatch you away...'

There was a faintly ironic undertone to his words that only Honor recognised. She flushed, remembering the lie that Helen had told him to avoid having to identify her sister.

'I...there wasn't one; Helen only said that because...' Her whisper staggered to a halt, her lips dragging against the pad of his thumb with every syllable in a way that was infinitely disturbing. She could actually taste him on her tongue.

'I *did* notice you weren't wearing a wedding-ring,' he informed her, staring at her mouth as if he knew how his thumb was making her feel. 'Is there anyone now who might feel impelled to take serious issue with your being here with me?'

'No, I——' Too late she realised the trap he had enticed her into. She took hold of his wrist and pulled his hand away from her face as she came back to the realisation of where they were. With a deft flick he twisted his hand in her grasp and firmly interlaced their fingers, grinning with an infuriating smugness as he pressed their joined hands to the snowy white tablecloth.

'Oh, yes, you're a real prince, Adam,' she said sarcastically. She wouldn't fall for that cunning seduction of her reason twice!

'Thank you, Honor.' He dipped his head and lifted their entwined hands to plant a kiss on her knuckles as he accepted her insulting play on words with gravely mocking sincerity. 'You flatter me with your kind homage. I'm glad to know that you consider me noble. It makes me feel worthy of a lady of gentle blood.'

Gentle blood? Her feelings towards him at the moment were anything but gentle! This time, when he lowered their hands he didn't stop at the table-top and Honor found the back of her hand trapped firmly against an iron-hard thigh.

She saw the two other women follow the motion with their eyes and was mortified. Did they think her hand was in his lap? Were they wondering what was going on under the table? Was Adam mad? Suddenly Joy looked up and Honor saw a wicked twinkle in her eye just as Tania let out an ear-splitting screech.

They all jumped, Tania overturning her chair as she backed away from the table.

'What is it?' Adam was on his feet, serious and instantly alert, his eyes going around the room. Honor's own heart was beating rather rapidly as she realised that, however relaxed his façade, the threats he had received must never be far from Adam's mind. She could almost see the adrenalin pumping through his veins.

'A rat!'

'A *rat*?' His vigilance turned to relieved annoyance. 'Is that all? You thought you saw a rat?'

'I didn't see it, I felt it!' Tania wailed, looking put out at his lack of concern. 'Something *horrid* and furry under the table. It *bit* me!' Tania displayed a pretty ankle strapped into a high-heeled sandal, revealing an appreciable amount of leg in the process. There was a neat set of reddening indentations at the back of her ankle. 'Look it's made a hole in my stocking. For God's sake,

Adam——' she hopped inelegantly further away from the danger zone '—it might have some horrible disease. Kill it!'

'Kill what?' Sara bounced back into the room in time to hear Tania's bloodthirsty demand.

Horrid and furry? That rang alarm bells. Honor lowered her feet cautiously from their safe perch on the rungs of her chair and ducked her head to take a peek under the tablecloth. Sure enough there sat Monty, tail lashing, looking disgustingly pleased with himself for the havoc he had created. For one cowardly moment Honor wondered whether she could quietly shoo him away and pretend innocence, but Sara's face had already appeared below the dangling tablecloth to inspect the culprit.

'It's probably the cat, that's all—hey, that's not Curry! It must be a stray. What are you doing under——? Ouch! It took a swipe at me!' She backed out and scrambled to her feet, sucking a finger. 'It's really wild. You must have stood on its tail or something, Aunt Tania...'

Her aggrieved aunt was still anxiously studying her bloodless wound. 'Now you know why I don't approve of animals in the house,' she snapped. 'If it's a stray it's probably brought fleas and who knows what disgusting diseases with it...'

'Monty, get out from under there,' Honor whispered urgently, taking a swipe at him with her foot to set him in motion before addressing Tania apologetically. 'I'm terribly sorry, Mrs Blake. It's my fault; I should have made sure my cat was—uh—secured in the kitchen. But he's very clean. He just has this habit of begging for left-overs——'

'*Your* cat?' If anything Tania was even more incensed. 'Adam, you mean to say you not only invited your...*friend* to stay without telling me, you also let her bring a *menagerie*——'

'One cat is hardly a menagerie,' Adam cut in, eyeing the furry friend now strolling nonchalantly out from his temporary lair. Unerringly Monty sought out his best chance of an ally, arching his back and purring innocently as Joy bent to pat and scold him fondly. 'Although on second thoughts I must admit that Monty does seem to cause as much trouble as a cartload of wild animals,' he added wryly.

'Is Monty the wildcat who gave you that scratch?' Sara guessed intuitively. The fresh indication of her lively intelligence made her dumbfounded initial reaction to Honor seem all the more inexplicable.

Adam grinned an acknowledgement at his daughter and he was suddenly the man from her letters again, warm and good-humoured, at ease with his feelings. The man she had instinctively trusted. Honor's confusion deepened, her instinct warring with her reason. She didn't really know him at all, she reminded herself.

'Adam, I said——'

'I heard what you said, Tania, and I suppose I assumed that as family I didn't need permission to make myself at home here. If we're going to quibble about trivialities, I might point out that you didn't ask if you could use my place this week while you were in town. You merely *informed* me that that was the most convenient thing for you to do.'

'The situation is hardly the same——' began Tania, haughty in her frustration.

'Quite. Technically I don't actually have to ask your permission for anything I choose to do here, since Zach saw fit to leave the house and farm property unconditionally to me.'

Tania hadn't inherited her husband's home! Had it been entailed in some way? Honor held her breath for an explosion. Adam's words had seemed like an unnecessarily cruel reminder of how much Tania had lost, but instead of exploding she seemed to soften, fluttering her impossibly long lashes at Adam's sardonic face.

'He knew how hopeless I was at managing things,' she said, smiling wistfully. 'He always said that if anything happened to him you'd take care of me. He trusted my future happiness and security to you, and so did I. So *do* I. It's just that I sometimes forget how much things have changed. That this is *our* home, not just *mine* any more...'

Honor admired the performance, as performance it undoubtedly was. Adam had just been skilfully reminded of his family obligations and sweetly dipped in guilt for his good fortune at the expense of the beautiful, helpless widow.

However, she noted that Adam looked remarkably guiltless as he glibly murmured an apology for his thoughtlessness.

'As a matter of courtesy, I would certainly have let you know about Honor's visit in advance—if I'd known about it myself. But it wasn't planned. I find that Honor is a very effective jinx where well-laid plans are concerned.' His eyelids drooped suggestively. 'The only way to circumvent the jinx is to take her by surprise. I didn't want her being alone in her house right now so I swept her off her feet and brought her here, where I knew she'd be safe under my protection. You might say I was overcome by my chivalrous instincts.'

That was too much for Honor. 'Chivalrous!'

He deflected her scorn with wicked amusement. 'All right, my passionate instincts, then.'

Honor was about to say something cutting about his passion when she remembered the tender ears tuned in their direction. Before she could rephrase her insult in suitably euphemistic terms Adam had moved to her side and grasped her elbow in the excruciatingly gentle hold with which he had earlier controlled her and began guiding her towards the door.

'As for your other uninvited guest, Tania, I'm afraid that Monty's every bit as assertive and unpredictable of temperament as his mistress, so I'd advise you to steer clear of him. Mum, perhaps you can coax him back into the kitchen, since you seem to be the only one he re-

spects. Honor and I have some business to discuss in
the study.'

'Business?' Tania's porcelain complexion was flushed
with an exquisite colour that Honor doubted was embarrassment. 'What kind of business? Adam—we
haven't had dessert yet and it's blackberry pie...your
favourite! I asked Rhonda to make it specially...'

Adam's smile positively smouldered as he glanced back
over his shoulder. 'You go ahead. Don't worry about
us. Honor and I will have our dessert in the study...'

CHAPTER SIX

'I HAVE a proposition for you.'

Honor stared at the man seated behind the heavy walnut desk. He might look perfectly sane, but he obviously wasn't. First his infuriating act at the dinner-table, and now this!

'The answer is no,' she said frigidly, crossing her legs to emphasise the firmness of her refusal. He had made her explain all over again about the misdirected letters while he listened, this time quietly and without expression, giving her hope that he was at last beginning to believe her. Instead he had probably been softening her up for some fresh outrage.

'You don't know what it is yet.'

He was rolling an elegant silver pen between strong fingers but his attention was elsewhere. Following his gaze, Honor saw the way that her dress had hiked up her thighs with her movement and she hurriedly uncrossed her legs, her chilly manner melting into flustered embarrassment. The man was a genius at unsettling her.

'I don't care what it is. The answer is still no.'

'Won't you at least hear me out? Surely you owe me that much.'

She sat straighter in her chair, mastering the quick flare of guilt. She wasn't going to be taken in by that plaintive air. The last time she had allowed herself to feel sorry for him she had got her drawers rifled.

'I don't owe you anything. Least of all consideration of some smutty proposition——'

The pen stopped rolling. 'What makes you think it's smutty?'

He sounded so surprised that she nearly blushed. Damn, she had almost given herself away there. When he had looked at her legs he had probably been imagining how much better Helen would have looked with a dress riding up her thighs.

'The way you carried on just now in the dining-room.' She used blistering sarcasm to cloak her injured pride. 'Hardly the perfect method of persuading your mother there's nothing between us!'

'Yes, well...I apologise for that,' he said meekly, meeting her gaze squarely. 'I guess I got a bit carried away with my desire for revenge. I'm sorry for teasing you.'

The handsome apology took the wind out of her billowing sails and they flapped emptily as she tried to maintain her defensive outrage.

'A *bit* carried away? You were practically drowning in your own drool!'

'How revoltingly descriptive,' he murmured drily, adding quickly as he saw her bristle, 'but very apt. You have a very strong attachment to colourful metaphors, don't you, Honor? You use rather a lot of them in your letters...'

The reminder of all that was between them brought her up short as she tried to remember exactly what revealing metaphors she might have used in the full flood of her creative outpourings. She had never edited her letters the way she edited her professional copy, she had just opened the floodgates of her imagination and let it flow.

'I knew it was just an act,' she said, wanting to make it clear that she hadn't been taken in for one moment by his behaviour in the dining-room; that she hadn't felt a single *frisson* of delight when he had touched her, kissed her hand, pressed it to his thigh...

'Of course you did,' he soothed. 'You're a very shrewd and intelligent woman. Far too intelligent to hold a grudge over a petty act of one-upmanship.'

'There's no need to go over the top,' she told him sourly. 'What is this proposition of yours, then?'

'A business one, naturally.'

Naturally. Honor didn't let her chagrin show.

'Go on,' she said, determined to refuse what was probably only a thinly disguised bribe for her to keep her mouth shut.

'I'm currently trying to sort out the mess my brother's death created in the family company. Unfortunately, while Zach was a born farmer it seems he wasn't much of a manager. It's partly my fault, because after our original expansion we ran things very much in tandem until my wife died. Zach oversaw the agricultural side, I worked the business angle. We all lived here then, so Tania got to play the lady of the manor to the hilt while Mum ran the household and Mary devoted herself to Sara...'

As if sensing Honor's sharpened interest, Adam rose and turned to the curtained window behind him, his hand going out to draw aside the velvet fabric before dropping back to his side in a gesture of clenched frustration. With a jolt Honor realised that he had probably been warned to stay away from lighted windows. He didn't turn around as he continued.

'Mary loved it here, but after her death I felt suffocated by the memories here so Sara and I moved to the city and I concentrated on building up the property-development company that I'd started as a sideline to our main interests. If I'd known Zach was struggling I would have helped but he never indicated that there were any problems or objected to my gradually withdrawing from active involvement in the management. He was my big brother. I'd always respected and admired him. Maybe he didn't want to jeopardise that, or maybe he didn't want to burden me with obligations that I'd clearly opted out of...'

Honor was wondering where his confidences were leading. She had the feeling that he was talking more to himself than to her as he sifted through his feelings.

'You mean your family company is in financial trouble?' she asked cautiously.

It was the wrong question to ask. He swung around, his body stiffening with threat. 'No, that's not what I mean. The company is basically sound, and if you print a word to the contrary I'll have a libel suit slapped on you so fast you'll wonder what hit you.'

She blinked. 'If you trust me that little, why on earth are you telling me all this?'

He scowled. It was something his harshly attractive face was very good at.

'All Blake Investments needs to get back on track is some firm direction from the top,' he said, ignoring her question. 'My first task is to get everyone motivated and enthusiastic. I want to draw the employees together and make them feel as if they have a real stake in the future of the company, whatever their job level. I want a staff newsletter, something slick but relatively inexpensive. But it'll take time to set up an in-house operation and I want this out *now*. I don't want to have to muck around with advertising agencies or submissions—this has to be seen to originate with *me*. I need someone on the spot with a proven expertise in desk-top publishing, someone who I know won't let me down...'

The light dawned. She got to her feet to confront him with her disbelief. 'You want *me*?'

His mouth twisted. 'In a manner of speaking. Why so incredulous—aren't you good at your job?'

'Of course I am. But you can't expect me to believe that you want someone you think has cheated and betrayed your confidence to work for you——'

'I thought I had apologised for that.'

'You apologised for smarming all over me at dinner,' she corrected him tartly.

'Smarming?' The twist turned into a smile. 'Is there such a word?'

'There is now.' She refused to be diverted by that calculated charm. 'You didn't apologise for everything else you've done.'

He shook his head. 'You're a hard woman, Honor Sheldon.'

'And you're a hard man.'

'Not yet, but keep provoking me and you'll find out just how hard I can get.'

He might not have meant the sexual innuendo but that didn't stop Honor's wayward glance downwards. As soon as she realised what she had done her eyes jerked back up his body, flushing as she met his knowing amusement.

'I didn't mean that kind of provocativeness, darling,' he murmured, driving her idiocy home.

'Don't call me that!'

'You called *me* darling.'

'Yes, but I was just....'

'Playing up to me. Yes, I know. Very reckless of you. Who taught you to flirt—your beautiful sister?'

A hot wave of unaccustomed jealousy washed over her. 'Leave Helen out of this!'

'Difficult, but I'll try. If you'll try and forgive me for not believing your obviously unsullied innocence.'

'What makes you assume I'm unsullied?' she snapped furiously, still burning over the implied comparison with Helen. 'I am twenty-five, you know. Just because I'm not blonde and drop-dead gorgeous doesn't mean I haven't had plenty of chances——'

This time his amusement burst into open mirth. His laughter was like warm sunlight in the shrouded room. It seemed his positive emotions were every bit as powerful as his negative ones.

'I'm sure you have, but I wasn't referring to your sexual experience, Honor. For a writer you do seem to have a terrible problem with misinterpretation of the language, don't you? I simply meant that the more time I spend in your company, the less I'm inclined to believe that you'd ever get involved in anything as dishonourable as extortion. You're rather well-named, I think.'

He tilted his head, regarding her simmering uncertainty thoughtfully. 'Did you know your eyes narrow when you lie... or, should I say, when you *try* to lie? As if you're screwing up your eyes along with your courage to do something that goes deeply against the grain. Actually it looks rather sexy. Innocent, but sexy, if you know what I mean.'

She didn't. She glared at him. Somehow he even managed to make a flattering assessment of her honourability sound like an insult so she offered him one in return. 'You have a twisted mind.'

'Because I said you have a sexy squint?'

'Yes—I mean, no—look, would you mind returning to the subject?'

'My proposition?' It sounded just as indecent as ever.

'Your offer of a *job*,' she clarified tightly. 'If it even exists, and wasn't just invented as a kind of trick——'

His eyes were suddenly as cool and assured as his tone. 'The job is very real, I assure you. If the police want you to stay here for a few days, why shouldn't we seek an advantage from the situation? I can arrange for your computer and files to be brought over and you can set up temporary office in one of the spare rooms. If you need a better reason to accept, why not consider doing some extra freelance work for me a fair exchange for a few days' room and board?'

Honor planted her fists on her hips. 'Fair? Don't think I'm going to barter away my services for virtually nothing! If I do your newsletter you're going to get billed in the usual way, at the usual rates. I was invited into this house as a guest, remember, and guests don't have to pay for room and board!' she informed him with relish, too busy enjoying scoring a point off him to realise the trap she had fallen into.

His eyes lowered so that she could not see their triumphant gleam. 'I can see that you don't need any advice from me about playing the advantage.'

'No, I don't. I'm not a babe in the woods. I've been looking after myself for a long time,' she told him stoutly.

'Is that because you don't get on with your family... with your sister?'

Helen again! 'Of course I do,' she snapped, 'but Mum and Helen love living in New York and I don't. Five years was enough for me. It was too big, too impersonal. So after I graduated from high school I persuaded Mum to let me come back here to live with Dad.'

'Your parents are divorced?'

'My father died a few years ago but no, they weren't. They just happened to want to live in two different countries. Mum chaperoned Helen and another teenage model when they won their first New York contracts and since I was only twelve and Dad was working erratic hours she took me with her. We just sort of stayed on when Helen's career took off but Dad was adamant he'd never leave New Zealand. He was the editor of the paper I work for...'

She braced herself for a mocking accusation of nepotism but it didn't come. Which was fortunate, for her father *had* created a job for her when she had first arrived back, an eager seventeen-year-old who hadn't quite known what she wanted to do with her life, except that somehow it would involve writing.

Luckily she had found her niche quite quickly, her high-school interest in computers and graphic art proving unexpectedly useful when the newspaper's owner had decided to switch to the new computerised technology. When her father died and the owner's son had rationalised the string of Auckland papers he owned she had been happy to accept the suggestion that she work directly from her home, since by then she was already doing quite a bit of freelance work via her home computer.

'So ink is in your blood. Didn't you ever want to be a model like Helen?'

Honor closed her eyes with a small shudder of genuine horror. 'God, no! Even if I'd had the build for it I didn't have the nerve. Models may look as if they've got delicate skins but really they need a hide like a rhinoceros to survive the criticism that's heaped on them day in, day out.'

'So you're the thin-skinned one in your family?'

For a big man he moved quietly. His finger sliding down the soft ridge of her collarbone made her eyes fly open.

'I was just wondering whether your scratches were still tender,' he said innocently, removing his finger from the anxious leap of her pulse in the hollow of her throat as he towered over her. 'You're lucky they don't show so you don't have to answer awkward questions.'

She clamped a hand to the soft-knit bodice of her dress, spreading it defensively across her breasts even though his eyes hadn't moved from her face. 'They're fine,' she said sternly, to banish the sly image of that lightly calloused fingertip dipping into her cleavage.

'I wasn't going to look,' he soothed, not moving away. 'I was merely showing friendly concern for a colleague.'

'I haven't said I'll take the job yet,' she denied skittishly.

He looked at her steadily for a moment, then sighed, his face hardening.

'I might have known it would come to this. I suppose you want exclusive rights to the inside story on the extortion when it breaks. Since you're already in possession of potentially damaging information you must know I'm hardly in a position to refuse.'

She blinked at him, her heart pattering uncomfortably fast under her splayed fingers as she contemplated an idea that hadn't even occurred to her. Still, it wouldn't do to let him know that...

'That would be blackmail,' she said slowly.

'I don't suppose that'll stop you using it to get what you want,' he said grimly. 'You know you have me over the proverbial barrel.'

Did she? Honor's eyes brightened from murky sea-green to emerald at this refreshing new perspective on the situation. Suddenly Adam's height and breadth and bullish determination didn't seem so intimidating. She lowered her protective hand, a slow smile breaking across her face, illuminating it with a soft glow of delighted discovery.

'So I do.' Her tone was redolent with smug satisfaction.

A muscle flexed along his hard jaw as he watched her former nervous unease smothered by a jaunty self-confidence.

'So?' The sullen challenge quivered slightly, no doubt with suppressed rage at his helplessness, thought Honor naïvely. The novelty of power rushed recklessly to her head.

'Sooo...' She drew out the word tauntingly. 'Maybe my working for you is going to turn out to be more expensive than you anticipated—a *lot* more expensive...'

He growled fiercely in his throat, his eyes glittering with more of that same, unidentified emotion. 'You ruthless little bitch!'

The gravelly insult gave her a sharp, illicit thrill. No one had ever called 'good old Honor' a bitch, let alone a ruthless one. She was too pleasant, too ordinary, too nice to excite anybody to strong feelings. An image of herself as a dangerous villainess conquering the superior strength of her masculine prey with brilliant strategems stalked across her brain, strongly appealing to her damaged ego.

'Tut, tut, Adam, calm down,' she said sweetly. 'You wanted me. You've got me. You just got a bit more of me than you bargained for!

'Now——' She strolled around his desk and flopped into his large swivel chair. The smooth leather was still warm from his body and accepted her generous contours with the barest of creaks. 'Why don't you sit down and give me the details?'

She waved him condescendingly into the guest seat, not surprised when he balked. She didn't quite have the gall to plant her feet on his desk-top but she made her point by picking up the pen he had been playing with earlier and studying it acquisitively as she rocked back in the chair.

'Nice pen. A gift?'

'For my birthday.' He paused, ruefully eyeing the she-devil his challenge had unleashed. She was stroking the blunt end of his pen slowly back and forth against her parted lips, leading him to wonder whether she had meant to tease him with the provocative sexual imagery that sprang irresistibly to mind.

Probably not. In spite of the innate sensuality revealed in her writing and in her impulsive response to stimuli he had the feeling that she didn't think of herself as sexy. In fact she was tormenting him with all the artless delight of a little girl playing dress-up in her big sister's clothes.

He chose his next words carefully, fascinated to discover how long she could sustain the act.

'Yes. From Sara. She saved up her pocket money for two months to buy it.'

He watched Honor drop the pen like a hot coal.

'Oh!' Honor felt like a worm as Adam suddenly changed his mind and took the seat his pride had rejected moments earlier. He raked a hand through his thick blond mane in an abstracted gesture of concern.

'But then, Sara's always been like that—very giving towards those she loves. I wish like hell that she hadn't chosen this particular moment to rebel but I know that it must be important to her... more important than the bit of schoolwork she'll miss. She can always make up time on her lessons but if I don't encourage her to confide her problems to me now I might regret it later on. I also know from experience that she won't tell me until *she's* ready.

'I can't hurt her by brushing her aside until it's more convenient for me. She wouldn't understand. And if she's here around the clock I'll have to explain what's going on because she's too clever not to sense something's wrong. Since Mary died she's been very sensitive to any threat to us as a family. I'll have to make it very clear that the anonymous letters are so far aimed at the company rather than me personally...'

Honor felt even lower than a worm. Of all the times to taunt a man with his helplessness this must surely be the worst! He had only been trying to protect his home and family. If only there was a way for her to make up for her thoughtless behaviour...

'Do you know for sure that it's a radical animal rights group?' she asked tentatively.

'No—that's the problem.' He cupped his hands behind his head and stretched wearily, arching his back in a typical gesture of masculine unselfconsciousness, the sides of his jacket sliding back, his shirt tautening over his wide chest, revealing a wedge-shaped shadow of dark hair beneath the thin white linen. Honor averted her eyes, rationalising the sudden prickle of sensual awareness that enveloped her body like a rash. She had felt intimately connected with this man for three months. It was quite natural that she should experience a physical curiosity about him. Natural and regrettably inappropriate!

'It's either a newly formed splinter group of fanatics or someone using the animal rights angle as a blind,' he continued, swinging his arms back down, his gaze fortunately aimed somewhere above her flustered head. 'The fact that they've mentioned money rather than

demanding Blake Investments stop poultry processing
supports the theory that it's a criminal rather than pol-
itical action. But it's all so damned *vague*! It's been over
two weeks since the first letter came and we still haven't
received a concrete demand, just speculation about what
could happen if we don't co-operate with any demands
they *might* make. Whoever it is seems to be more intent
on prolonging the agony than taking the money and
running.'

His eyes dropped suddenly to her face and he studied
her concerned expression for a moment before saying
with an edge of angry frustration still in his voice, 'If
this is our first interview shouldn't you be taking notes?
By all means feel free to use my pen...'

Honor flushed, caught off guard yet again. 'Surely
I'm entitled to some personal curiosity... considering
the fact that I was a suspect.'

'You still are.' As her dark brows dragged raggedly
together he added blandly, 'We're all suspects as far as
the police are concerned. Even me.'

'You!' She regarded him with fresh shock, her annoyance on her own behalf forgotten.

He shrugged. 'I might be trying to perpetrate an in-
surance fraud or cover up an embezzlement...'

'No wonder the police haven't tracked anyone down
yet,' Honor cried hotly, leaping out of the seat of power
to pace impatiently around the desk. 'They're too busy
chasing after ridiculous red herrings. Surely they can't
believe you'd be involved in such a ludicrously stupid
plan!'

'Thank you, Honor, for your trust——'

'It's not a matter of trust, it's a matter of common
sense,' she cut him off flatly. 'If you were embezzling
you wouldn't draw attention to yourself like this. You're
too clever. You'd do it in such a cunning way that nobody
would ever find out, let alone suspect you.'

'Thank you again... I think.'

His irony pierced her outraged self-absorption on his behalf. Honor stopped pacing and stared down at him. 'Well... it's simply ridiculous,' she finished lamely.

'So you said. If I ever need a character witness, remind me not to pick you. You're likely to incriminate me with the enthusiasm of your defence.'

As if she hadn't already caused him enough trouble today on top of all his real woes, she thought guiltily. 'I was just thinking aloud. I wouldn't say things like that to the police,' she said hurriedly, her small, capable hand automatically patting the broad shoulder nearest to her reassuringly as she added darkly, 'I know what it's like to be an innocent under suspicion.'

'Thank you,' he repeated with the same thread of sardonic amusement. A warm hand wrapped around her wrist, holding her palm against the heavily shifting muscle as he tipped his head back. 'You're awfully gullible, aren't you, Honor?'

'Gullible?'

'Susceptible to emotional pressure. Easily distracted from your purpose.'

Her generous mouth tightened, sensing something unpleasant coming. He made her sound disgustingly feeble.

'I don't think so,' she denied firmly. Her captured fingers curled into the rough weave of his jacket. He was beginning to make an unwelcome habit of shackling her to his side while he took point-blank pot-shots at her character.

'You were all set to screw me for every cent you could get until I reminded you I had a daughter,' he pointed out, 'then all your hostility melted like ice in the sun. How on earth does someone as tender-hearted as you stand up for herself in the real world?'

It was too late to save face but she made a valiant try to outface his callous opportunism.

'Don't think I still won't,' she said fiercely.

'Won't what? Screw me?' The tiny white lines around his eyes and mouth disappeared into the smoothly tanned skin as he grinned with wicked complacency.

'With pleasure!' she snapped, desperately wanting to wipe the smirk off his face. Instead he shouted with laughter and she belatedly recognised the crudity of his remark and the indecency of her response. She jerked her hand out of his and backed up against the desk. Now he would think her even more idiotically naïve.

'I look forward to the experience,' he chuckled. 'I'm glad you're working with me rather than against me. In troubled times like this a man likes to know he has an utterly ruthless bitch like you on his side.'

'I hope you don't use language like that around your daughter,' she said quellingly, his words a clear indication that the emotion he had been so obviously suppressing earlier had been amusement rather than anger. He hadn't feared her any more than a lion feared a feckless fawn. He had been callously leading her on, playing heartlessly on her sympathy—and she had fallen for it—again!

'No, ma'am,' he affirmed gravely, his tawny eyes still dancing with insufferable mockery. She wanted to smack him. Her hands clenched on the desk-top behind her as she struggled to control the violent impulse.

Maybe it was a good thing that she had allowed herself to be manoeuvred into this ignominious situation, she thought furiously, striving to find a bright side to her gloomy situation. So it hurt to discover that he was laughing at her... good! After foolishly falling in love with an imaginary hero, a harsh dose of infuriating reality was exactly what she needed to halt the creeping rot. She would hang around just long enough for propinquity to do its dirty, disillusioning work and then she would walk out, heart-whole and pride intact—not to mention financially better off!

And, of course, while she was here she would be living in the lap of luxury. She probably wouldn't have to lift a finger around the house. She would also be putting Tania's snooty nose thoroughly out of joint, sweet revenge for being treated like something the cat had dragged in. It would almost be worth the inevitable strife for that pleasure alone! Then there was the opportunity for a journalistic coup, although it was hardly a tribute to her professionalism that the prospect of a scoop came a poor second to the chance of thoroughly annoying one of the rural aristocracy.

She listened broodingly as Adam briskly outlined the terms under which she was to stay, which included her sharing the elementary safety precautions the family had adopted on police advice. Whether she was on the property or off it, she had to make sure that at least one other person in the household knew where she was at all times.

'Since I don't have my bicycle and my car is still being fixed I don't see myself being able to venture very far,' she said truculently. Everything he said sounded so reasonable that she knew there had to be a catch but, try as she might, she couldn't find it.

'There's usually at least one of the farm vehicles around at any given time. If you go down to the orchard office in the paddock behind the house and ask, I'm sure someone will find the time to run you where you want to go,' Adam said equably. 'I'll mention it to Dave—he's our orchard manager. However, try and keep it down to essential trips and don't tell all and sundry where you're staying. It's bad enough that Tania won't take it seriously and keeps flitting off, but then she was ever one for burying her head in the sand to avoid facing unpleasantness.'

Honor looked at him in disbelief. That certainly hadn't been her impression. Tania had been all for burying *her* in unpleasantness!

'She doesn't want me here,' she said bluntly, wondering exactly what his feelings for his glamorous sister-in-law were.

'As I pointed out to her earlier, owning this house gives me certain privileges. Tania will just have to grin and bear it,' he replied evenly.

Honor felt a twinge of unwelcome sympathy for the woman. After all, she was probably just fighting for her own security in the only way she knew how. If her only training had been as a pampered wife and social butterfly, how else was she supposed to cope with the dramatic changes Zach's death had brought?

'Whoever owns it, this is still her home. She's entitled to resent me barging in...'

'Resent, yes, dictate, no. Don't invest Tania with your own sentimentality. She has no emotional attachment to the land or this place. She was always trying to get Zach to move closer to town. If he had left it to her she would have sold a three-generation-old farm in a flash and bought something along Auckland's wildly inflated golden mile. But she's not poverty-stricken by a long chalk. She knows damned well she could buy something in the city tomorrow if it suited her. So don't fall into the trap of feeling sorry for her. Tania can well look after herself, in spite of her indications to the contrary.'

'So why does she stay?' she asked challengingly.

He gave her a droll look as he rose lazily to his feet. 'Why, Honor, like you she finds me utterly irresistible and thinks propinquity might succeed where artful dissembling failed!'

Lying awake in bed a few hours later, Honor was still trying to come up with a crushing response to his arrogant throw-away remark. She should have flung at him that they obviously had radically different theories on the effects of propinquity! Lumping her in with Tania was enough of an insult. How dared he joke about what to Honor was a thoroughly mortifying situation? What made him think he was so irresistible, anyway?

Honor shot bolt upright in the bed, her eyes wide with horror in the darkness.

Her letters!

She *knew* there had been something nagging at the back of her mind. She *knew* there had been an important issue she had meant to settle before she agreed to anything. But she had been side-tracked by his conniving.

She had forgotten to ask for her letters back. It didn't seem fair that he was the only one to be able to redeem his embarrassment. Good God, what if he decided to read through them again? What if he re-read all that drivel she had written to the man of her dreams? As long as those words were held hostage over her head she would never have peace of mind.

Honor looked towards the firmly closed door that connected her room with his. A thin white line illuminating the bottom edge of the wood told her he was still awake.

A strange urgency took hold of her. She wasn't going to wait until the morning to settle this. She would never get to sleep for worrying about it.

She scrambled out of bed, dislodging Monty who had been curled up on her feet, gently snoring, and headed for the beckoning slit of light, swerving off course when she caught sight of her shimmering reflection in the mirror. The pale satin sleep-shirt was buttoned to the collarbone and a perfectly respectable knee-length, but she was taking no chances. Adam wasn't going to get an excuse to claim she was coming on to him, even as a joke.

Remembering something she had seen in the wardrobe when she had tucked away her motley collection of clothes, she opened it up and took out the old-fashioned, faded red cloth coat. Securing its voluminous folds around her with the matching tie belt, she grimaced as she checked again in the mirror. She looked as if she was wearing a carpet. Still, no one would dare to accusing her of vamping.

There was no answer to her tentative knock at his door so she knocked again a little louder.

'Adam? Can I come in? I have to speak to you.'

She couldn't hear a sound from the other side but somehow she was certain he was there, deliberately letting her stew.

She knocked sharply once more and called out warningly, 'I'm coming in!' before easing open the door, and cautiously peeping in.

The room was empty, the bedside light bouncing off the crisp white sheets that were invitingly turned down, the brass bed-rails gleaming with a polished sheen.

'Adam?'

Honor ventured inside, checking behind the door but curbing the sudden impulse to lift the edge of the quilt and look under the bed. She put a hand across her mouth to stem a nervous giggle. It was like being a child again, bravely searching the bedroom every night for bogey-men before she took a flying leap into the safety of her bed. She had believed even then that it was better to face a fear than try to hide from it.

She looked around, noticing that the only photograph in the room was one of Sara. There seemed to be none anywhere in the house of his precious Mary—as if he couldn't bear the reminder of what he had lost. He must have been very much in love with her. Perhaps he still was and that was why he had sought solace in letter-writing—the temptation to be unfaithful to his memories was less...

'Sleep-walking, Honor?'

She gasped and spun around. Adam had silently entered from the hall. He wore a calf-length, black towelling robe with red piping along the lapels and edges of the belt, and was rubbing his wet hair with a bath-towel. She tried not to notice that the thicket of dark gold hair on his chair also needed drying, jewel-like sparkles of moisture sliding through the furry coils as he padded barefoot across the room.

'I've decided I want to have my letters back too,' she stated baldly, before he could jump to any arrogant conclusions about her presence in his bedroom.

He gave his head one final flurry and threw the towel across a stool, raking both hands carelessly through his damp hair as he turned to her. 'Now?'

'Well ... yes ... if they're here—if you still have them, that is...' She realised her floundering was providing him with ready-made excuses and quickly changed her tune. 'Yes, now, please.'

'Hmm ... I wonder what the legal position on ownership of voluntary correspondence is? It's probably a simple matter of possession....'

She folded her arms across the moth-eaten coat and glared at him. 'I gave you yours when you asked.'

'So you did.' His lips quirked as he suddenly registered her eccentric attire but fortunately for his health he didn't comment. 'I'll see if I can find them.'

'You do that,' said Honor sourly. *His* robe bore a Givenchy symbol, embroidered on the pocket. I'll bet it was a gift, she thought, watching him open a drawer in the tall, antique bureau in the corner. A man who didn't notice his socks were mismatched and used his fingers instead of a comb didn't seem to be the type to bother with vanity bathroom-wear. On the other hand the robe suited him perfectly, she acknowledged ruefully, the black a perfect foil for his blond hair and tanned skin.

'Here you are. Would you mind telling me what the urgency is?'

Honor picked up the bundle of envelopes he had tossed carelessly on to the bed. They were held together by a rubber band—scarcely romantic—but at least he'd kept them. Honor counted roughly and caught her breath when she realised what he was trying to do.

'And the rest!' she cried. 'Come on, Adam, where are the last half-dozen I wrote? You know they're the ones I'm talking about...'

He raised a quizzical eyebrow. 'Do you get the feeling we've played this scene before—with roles reversed?'

She gritted her teeth. 'Very funny. Now you've had your little joke at my expense, how about handing them over?' When he continued to regard her oddly she exploded. 'I might have known you wouldn't play fair!' She thrust the letters into the coat's sagging patch-pocket and marched across to the bureau to tug at the drawer he had delved into. It opened a tiny crack then jammed as it hit a solid, black-robed hip.

'They're not in there, Honor——'

'Well, where are they, then?' she demanded belligerently. He was giving her that blank-eyed look that she had already come to hate, the one that meant he was stalling for time while his swift intelligence plotted to outwit her.

'Are you thinking of trying to blackmail me? Don't you find that terribly ironic in the circumstances? Well, you can forget it. They're really not that important.'

Perhaps her lofty lie pricked his conscience, for his stance relaxed.

'I'll get them for you, Honor, I promise.' With a deft nudge of his hip he thrust the drawer closed again and hooked a finger under her belt. 'Just not tonight. Really...it's late and I'm tired.' He towed her stiffly resisting body back around the bed.

Her little snort told him what she thought of his promises.

'When?' she demanded.

'Soon.'

She dug in her heels, grabbing the end rail of the bedstead as he tried to manoeuvre her to the door. 'How soon?'

His mouth compressed at her stubbornness and his fingers twisted impatiently in her belt. 'As soon as I can get to them. Now why don't you go back to bed——?'

'Get to them?' All her senses went on alert at his slip. 'Where are they? Don't tell me you gave them to the *police*?' she wailed in mortification.

'No, of course not. Look, Honor, I——' Something gave between them and they both looked down in surprise. The aged belt had parted under the pressure of his strong fingers and with nothing to anchor it the thick coat curled apart under its own formidable weight.

There was a tiny silence. Adam was first to recover.

'Rolling out the red carpet for me, Honor?' he murmured softly, his metaphor revealing how dangerously attune to her thoughts he was. He fingered a fold of slippery, butter-coloured satin. 'Isn't this rather demure, given your wicked taste in lingerie?'

Her mouth felt strangely dry. 'You were the one who did my packing,' she pointed out croakily, fascinated by the contrast between the shiny-smooth fabric and the hair-roughened back of his hand. She should step away, she knew she should. This was terrible. Exactly the sort of thing she had wanted to avoid!

'Very sensuous, though . . .' He flattened his hand against the front of her shoulder and created a soft friction between the fabric and her skin, the warmth of his touch sinking to her very bones. She felt a vivid tingling in her breasts and suddenly there were jagged shoals forming under the slick satin.

'And maybe not so demure,' he growled, watching the change take place. Where the fabric had formerly flowed over her breasts in a smooth unbroken curve, it now fell from two prominent peaks which trembled with each uncertain breath she took. His hand moved down and suddenly he was weighing her in his large palm, his fingers curving under her breast to her ribs while his thumb rode the upper swell. 'Look how perfectly you fill my hand . . .'

Honor bit her lip to stop herself moaning at his throaty murmur of gratified discovery of her size. His thumb moved experimentally against the thinly sheathed peak and this time the sound escaped her control, along with an explicit shiver that arced along her nerves, transmitting an unmistakable message to the man who held her.

His eyes smouldered, the sensuous curiosity in his expression hardening to savage satisfaction.

'Oh, yes, you like that, don't you, Honor? You like the way I can make you feel...'

With his other hand he reached around and took hold of the collar of the coat, peeling it down her body and kicking it away from their feet as his fingers returned to stroke warmly up the sensitive back of her thigh. The satin hem ruffled against his forearm as he ventured further, teasing the soft downiness of her bottom. With a thick groan he spanned the twin globes with the broad cup of his hand, adjusting his stance to pull her tightly between his legs as he found her mouth and set the seal on her pleasure with his kisses.

The taste of him was as recklessly novel and exciting as his touch and Honor stopped lying to herself and threw caution to the winds. She wrapped her arms around his neck and went on tiptoe to fit herself closer to the hard male contours. The hem of his robe parted as he accommodated himself to her need, her hands clenching in the silky dampness of his hair as she felt the naked rasp of thick, hard thighs against her own. They were as densely furred as his chest, taut and quivering with the same rigid, muscular tension. Only the secure knot at his waist shielded her from blatant awareness of his burgeoning arousal. The threat of that reality muted, Honor was free to indulge her forbidden fantasies. She twisted her torso, seeking to increase the contact but not wanting to trap his hand and stop the exquisitely sweet torment at her breast; she opened her mouth and mind and heart to the luxury of pure, unadulterated, concentrated sensation.

He responded to her lack of inhibition with a violent surge of lust. Both hands now cupped her bottom, his fingers curving deep into the dimpled flesh as he held her still for the heated thrusting of his hips. His tongue was equally fierce in the silky moistness of her mouth, shocking her with his ability to make her feel full and empty at the same time.

Only when he pushed her on to the bed and bent his head to fiercely suckle her breast through the cream satin did her sensual stupor begin to dissipate. She suddenly became frighteningly aware of Adam's powerfulness, his nudity beneath the robe. Even two overlapping layers of double towelling could no longer disguise the full extent of his swollen arousal. She badly wanted him to finish what they had started, for him to make love to her, but what Adam wanted undoubtedly had very little to do with that emotion. If nothing else, tonight had proved that he had a very strong sex drive. If he was still tied up in knots about his wife it was no wonder he had gone off the deep end.

She felt his hand touch her belly and caught her breath on a wave of delicious weakness. 'Adam——' Her feeble protest was drowned by a loud crash from her room, quickly followed by a softly galloping thunder.

'What the——?' Adam's eyes were glazed and his cheekbones streaked with red as he jerked his head up, instinctively wrenching Honor off the bed and pushing her protectively behind him, away from the source of the noise.

The door to her room shuddered wider. A flash of grey streaked between their feet and shot out of the other door, leaving them teetering.

'Monty!'

The realisation came simultaneously, although only Adam added raggedly, 'That scrawny cat! What's he done now? One day he's going to go too far and I'm going to wring his bloody neck!'

His curse had a delightfully permanent sound to it but Honor was too busy staring, slack-jawed, after Monty. The hall door—it had been open all the time! Honor

went hot and cold as she contemplated what could have
happened. Thank God it had only been Monty who had
witnessed their lustful clinch!

No sooner had the prayer gone up than a slender figure
in a striking négligé appeared at the door enquiring about
the noise, and then a smaller one wearing what looked
like a dead ringer for the discarded red carpet.
Tania and Joy.

And, then, the final blow—a child. Sara. As wide-
eyed as ever and even more inquisitive.

Being discovered together in a mutual state of undress
would never have got a conviction—after all, everybody
summoned by the crash was wearing her night-things.
The violent upheaval of the sheets *could* have been the
result of an early nightmare and the tousled hair and
flushed expressions might *just* have been evidence of a
vigorous argument in progress.

What really destroyed Honor's reputation in the Blake
household as a woman of accepted virtue were two things
that only a child would have dreamed of drawing attention to.

Why, Sara asked, did Honor have a small, transparent wet patch on a strategically important part of her
nightshirt, and why was her father 'walking funny'?

CHAPTER SEVEN

HONOR bit into a big, crisp red apple, grateful for the techniques of modern cool storage which allowed her to enjoy such a fresh, sweetly ripe taste when all around her were trees laden with tiny, bitterly sour green fruit.

She sighed with content as she munched, lying back in the cropped grass under the shifting shade of the shelter-belt trees. The tall, leafy species, planted to protect the fruit-bearing trees and kiwi-fruit vines from the wind, provided the perfect, peaceful resting spot. She closed her eyes, savouring the sounds of the country. Even the distant buzz of a tractor seemed strangely in tune with the environment.

Her peace was short-lived.

'What are you doing down here? Are you hiding?'

The girl must have radar. Honor opened her eyes reluctantly. Sara stood over her, panting, her round face pink and glossy from the exertion of running, her pale hair escaping from the rudimentary ponytail straggling crookedly from the side of her head. She wore grass-stained jeans, a shrill T-shirt and an expression of smug satisfaction. She couldn't have looked more scruffy if she had tried... and Honor guessed that she must have tried very hard, for the previous afternoon Tania had produced an unexpected gift for her 'favourite only niece'—a clutch of dainty dresses that she thought Sara might like to wear around the house.

'I'm having my lunch. What are you doing—come for a sly smoke?' She had had four days to get over the shock of being painted a scarlet woman, time enough to find a surprisingly natural ease in the girl's company.

Sara giggled. She flopped down beside Honor. 'Dad's looking for you.'

113

'Is he?' Honor took another bite of her apple, endeavouring to appear hugely unmoved by the declaration when her pulse was leaping madly. Damn it, you would think by now that her body would have calmed down!

'Is that who you're hiding from? Dad? Why, what's he done?'

'I'm not hiding——'

'Then why aren't you having lunch up at the house with us? Granny said we can have it by the pool today. Did you know I won the school junior swimming championship? I bet I could beat you in a race.'

'I think you might have mentioned it a few times,' said Honor drily. If Sara wasn't asking frank and embarrassing questions she was force-feeding Honor unsolicited confidences. In a dramatic contrast to the sickly shock with which she had greeted Honor's arrival, she had now decided that her dad's new best friend must be *her* best friend.

And she was helpful, so helpful that Honor couldn't turn around in the upstairs drawing-room in which her computer had been set up as promised without being offered a cup of tea or coffee or finding her pencil newly sharpened or her copy removed from her printer and neatly trimmed of its perforated edges.

Not wanting to hurt any fragile adolescent feelings, Honor had made sure she always had some little job ready to be tackled, but she soon discovered that Sara's spirit was irrepressible. She wasn't crushed by being ignored or snapped at, or even at being told to shut up and go away. Like her father, the girl had an independent self-confidence that was almost impossible to shake. She believed in her ability to do anything she set her mind to. When she failed she only became more determined to succeed next time. It was exhausting to watch her.

'So, if you're not hiding from dad it must be Aunt Tania!'

That was too close to the mark. 'I told you, I'm not hiding, I'm having a picnic.'

'You don't have to worry, she's gone to some Growers' Association lunch,' said Sara helpfully. 'She was mad because Dad was supposed to be her escort but he said he didn't have time to take her. Is that apple all you're having? You're not trying to diet, are you? You shouldn't take any notice of what Aunt Tania says. Did you know she sometimes takes diet pills to keep thin? That's pretty obsessive, don't you think? They can be addictive, you know——'

'Like cigarettes, you mean?' Honor interrupted hastily. Whatever her own opinion of Tania, it was wrong to encourage Sara's disrespect towards her aunt. She was guiltily aware that by listening to the chatter in order to find out more about Adam's life she had provided tacit approval of Sara's eager indiscretions. Unfortunately on the one subject that Honor was *most* curious, and most reluctant to enquire about—Sara's mother—the girl had been utterly discreet.

Sara grinned, revealing teeth that were well-shaped but ever so slightly misaligned. She had refused to have braces—partly, Honor was sure, because Tania was so insistent on the importance of having perfect teeth.

'Actually I was nearly sick,' she confessed. 'I only did it to get sent home.'

So Adam was right. Honor tried to sound non-chalant. 'Oh? Why was that?'

For a moment she thought Sara was going to spill it out, then the girl shrugged sheepishly and picked at the grass around her feet.

'You should have a talk to your father; he's been worried about it,' Honor urged gently. 'Or your grandmother, if it's something to do with—er——'

'Sex? Nah, nothing like that,' Sara responded with a frankness that put Honor's waffling to shame. 'If it was that I could come to you, couldn't I?' she added slyly.

'Aunt Tania said that you're the expert on sex around here.'

The shady spot suddenly seemed stiflingly hot. 'You shouldn't eavesdrop on people, Sara,' said Honor in her best quelling voice.

'It's the only way to find the good stuff out when you're a kid,' said Sara, unquelled. 'Besides, I wasn't eavesdropping that time. Aunt Tania just said it kind of under her breath... only she was breathing pretty hard and it came out quite loud. Granny heard too.'

'And what did Granny say?' Honor couldn't help asking.

'She didn't say anything.' Sara frowned. 'Granny doesn't say much when Aunt Tania's around. She's afraid of getting things wrong in front of her. She forgets things sometimes, too... but just little things, not the important stuff. She likes being busy. She always used to cook when Dad and I came to visit, when Uncle Zach was alive, because Aunt Tania doesn't like messing around in the kitchen. Granny's been sick but she just had a cough and a bad cold. I don't think she has that disease that they put you in a home for—the A one...'

'Alzheimer's?'

'Yeah. Aunt Tania's got a book on it. Stories about people forgetting what day it is and who their family is and where they live. Granny's not like that. She still plays bowls and everything.'

'No, she's not like that,' said Honor firmly, wondering whether anxiety over her grandmother was the source of Sara's fears and annoyed with Tania for exposing her to that fear, however inadvertently. 'She's a warm, whimsical, spontaneous person,' she emphasised. All the things that Tania wasn't! 'I've had lots of chats with her and never noticed anything wrong. In fact she's always seemed as sharp as a tack under that fluffy smile...' Except for their first encounter, perhaps, but those initial, almost pathetically eager misconceptions had been set in concrete by the Bedroom Incident and Adam's subsequent irritating behaviour. But Honor didn't want to dwell on *that* . . .

'She only seems vague around your aunt, maybe because they don't get on and your granny doesn't like to get involved in arguments——'

'You mean because Aunt Tania bullies her?' said Sara bluntly.

Was Tania's behaviour that calculated? Honor hoped not.

'A lot of people like to think they know what's best for everyone else,' she said diplomatically. 'Especially with other people who are not as assertive as themselves. But they're not necessarily right just because they express themselves more forcefully. You couldn't get two people with a more different outlook on life than your aunt and your granny; that's probably why they have difficulty communicating. And then, too, maybe your aunt is afraid for your granny as she gets older—maybe she doesn't want to feel responsible if something happens while she's out.'

'She's always out . . . except when Dad's around,' Sara pointed out gruffly.

'If you're really concerned about it, why don't you mention it to your father . . . ?' Honor said hopefully.

'Oh, I already have, ages ago,' said Sara, shooting that grand theory down in flames. 'After Uncle Zach died. Dad said never, no way is he ever putting Granny in a home. And Aunt Tania doesn't have to worry about being responsible because Granny's coming to live with us . . . when Dad decides where we're going to live, that is, because we might be staying here . . .'

'Would you like that?' Honor asked, her heart misgiving at the thought of Adam living permanently near by. She'd be forever in dread of running into him, having to smile and pretend polite disinterest in his affairs . . .

Sara shrugged and smiled very cryptically for a girl who probably didn't know what the word meant. 'Maybe. It depends on how things work out . . .'

Honor opened her mouth to ask what things, but Sara beat her to it.

'Are you sure you won't come back to the house for lunch? After Aunt Tania left, Granny made a pizza and scones and apple muffins...'

Honor's mouth watered. She looked sadly down at her apple core. So much for will-power. 'Well...I'll have to have a swim afterwards.' If it hadn't been for the pool she would have put on kilos from the delicious meals she was eating.

'Great, I'll give you a race. Oh, look...I told you Dad was looking for you!' She jumped up and bounded out to meet the four-wheeled farm-bike that roared up from the bottom of the orchard, skidding to a stop at the nearest row of apple trees.

Honor couldn't hear what Adam said to his daughter over the roar of the motorcycle engine but she could see its effect. Sara laughed and tossed a mischievous look over her shoulder at Honor and began running back towards the house, making little darting leaps and hops over tufts of grass as she did so. She certainly had a lot of energy, thought Honor, getting up slowly, feeling hot and messy as she eyed the man who, after gunning the engine aggressively once more, leaned over and turned it off.

In the resultant silence the faint sound of the engine ticking over seemed unnaturally loud. Like a time bomb, thought Honor nervously.

'What are you doing out here?'

He and his daughter were definitely of like mind, only the same question from Sara hadn't made Honor bristle.

'Taking a break,' she said crisply. 'That's the whole point about working for yourself; you don't have to kowtow to a slave-driving boss.'

'But the newspaper must have deadlines that you have to meet,' he said mildly, unruffled by her challenge. 'And your clients must ask for their work to be done by a certain date.'

'I still work to my own schedule. I haven't had any complaints up until now.' She gave him a fierce look.

He lifted his hands off the bike's handlebars and spread them in a gesture of appeasement. Dressed in a faded short-sleeved shirt that hung open above his dusty denim jeans he looked the quintessential farm worker, from the scuffed boots to the battered felt hat. He looked fit, healthy and relaxed, a far cry from the raging bull she had first encountered.

'I'm not complaining. Quite the reverse. So far you've been doing a fabulous job.'

She wished she knew he was referring purely to the newsletter she was still piecing together. She had the feeling that he was speaking of another agenda entirely.

'I'd do an even better one if you'd stop interrupting me,' she said hardly.

She found it very difficult to concentrate on her screen when at any moment she could expect to look up and find Adam there, silently observing her with that expression of amused and faintly bewildered speculation that was so unnerving.

She didn't need to be checked up on and after their first discussion about his project he must have known it. But he still kept seeking her out with flimsy excuses, knowing what it must look like to the rest of the household, knowing how disturbing she found his persistent attention. Disturbing because she couldn't find the strength of mind to reject it.

The trouble was that living with him, working with him, wasn't providing the kind of cure that she had hoped. Learning about the other side of Adam, the side he had concealed in his letters, only compounded her problem. Yes, he was wretchedly stubborn and arrogant and argumentative, but he also bent like a willow for those he loved: off-beat and whimsical with his mother; a romping child with his daughter; firm and even kind, in an implacably cool sort of way, with Tania.

He was simply...Adam. And, God forbid, her be-
loved fantasy hero was beginning to pale in comparison
to the flesh and blood reality.

'I like to keep my finger on the pulse; that's why I
wanted you here while you worked on it,' Adam said
reasonably, interrupting her brooding thoughts. 'It's
good to have a constant exchange of ideas going on,
don't you think? Keeps the creative juices flowing.'

His eyes half masked by the shady brim of his hat,
drifted down the length of her in the loose, drop-waisted
summer shift which she had fetched, along with an
armload of other clothes, when Adam had driven her
back to her house to fetch her computer and files and
shut up the house properly. He frowned at the sight of
her bare feet.

'Where are your shoes? You shouldn't wander around
a working orchard without some foot protection. Have
you a current tetanus shot?'

'I had a booster a couple of years ago.' Honor bent
to pick up her sturdy canvas slip-ons from their hiding
place in the grass, and put them on. 'My father always
worked on country papers. I spent my childhood in the
country. It wasn't so long ago that I've forgotten the
rules. I just took them off when I sat down.'

'In that outfit you look as if childhood was only yesterday,' Adam said drily, crossing his arms on the chrome
stem of the handlebars and leaning forward to give her
another lazy survey. 'I'm sure Sara's summer school
uniform is almost exactly the same.'

'If you wanted glamour you should have gone to the
Growers' lunch with Tania,' Honor sniped back, regretting the jealous retort when Adam grinned.

'I didn't say I didn't like it. I've always been a sucker
for girls in uniform...Mary was a St John Ambulance
volunteer. Have you been pumping my darling daughter
about my activities?'

'No, I have not,' she said hotly, flirting marginally
with the truth as she pondered his rare reference to his

wife. Joy had mentioned Mary only a few times, always with a reverent expression, mentioning her loveliness and what a wonderful wife and mother she had been, and how Adam had put away all the photographs of her because they made him so sad. If Mary Blake had been as good as she was beautiful, no wonder no living woman could match up to her memory! 'I wish I could *stop* her telling me things.'

'Do you?' His scepticism was like a red rag to a bull. 'She likes you. You have the Sara seal of approval. Which is fortunate considering you're supposed to be madly in love with me.'

Honor drew a sharp breath before realising he was teasing. 'And whose fault is it that she thinks that? You shouldn't encourage her, Adam——'

'To like you?'

He was being deliberately obtuse. 'No, to laugh at your sister-in-law...to side with me against her. It—it isn't fair!'

'To whom? Tania? I doubt if she even realises it. She doesn't see Sara as a separate person in herself, just as adjunct to me. She never took a blind bit of notice of her before. I have no intention of being conned into playing Tania's lord and protector for the rest of my life so that she won't have to bother about life's tiresome practicalities, and the sooner she accepts it the better. Thankfully, I think the scales are finally falling from her eyes. Before she stormed out this morning she told me that Zach was worth fifty of me. The only pity was that marrying him had given her a selfish, overbearing, social retard for a brother-in-law!'

'Well, she got that right!' said Honor feelingly, shattered to have her suspicions so wretchedly confirmed. She had been the means to an end, that was all.

'Oh, I don't think of it as an end at all, Honor. I think of it as a new beginning,' he said blandly, making her realise that she had spoken aloud. 'You don't have a hat to go with those shoes, do you? That wild mop of hair is no protection from the sun and your nose is already looking a bit pink. It's a long walk back to the house. Hop on and I'll give you a ride. We don't want to be late for lunch.'

'Thanks, but I'll walk,' Honor bit out huffily. Suddenly she felt in need of a good cry.

'It'll be quicker on the bike. There's plenty of room.' He eased his pelvis forward and indicated the back of the curving seat.

'No, I——'

'Never been on one before? The four wheels make it very safe.'

'I'm not worried about that——'

'*I'm* very safe, too.' He tipped the brim of his hat to her in a parody of old-fashioned politeness.

'I'm sure you are,' Honor said tightly, her desire to cry evaporating in the heat of her rising temper. 'But I'd prefer to walk.'

'You're squinting, Honor. Is that the sun or are you telling fibs?' He laughed at her scowling expression. 'Come on, stop being such a ninny. You know you want to. It's hot and I'll bet you're dying of thirst. If you don't want to put your arms around me, I'll scoot back a bit and you can sit in front of me.' He watched her actually contemplate the option before adding wickedly, 'Between my legs. You'd feel *extra* safe then, Honor. You've been there before, remember, and emerged unscathed.'

'*That* is a matter of opinion,' Honor delighted him by muttering tartly. She reached out to touch the hot rubber of the huge, fat rear tyres. He was right, damn him, she *did* want to. She'd seen some of the orchard employees tearing around on the bikes and it had looked rather fun. Why should she deprive herself of an enjoyable new experience just to prove Adam wrong?

Getting on proved a little more complicated than he had implied. Honor had to hitch her skirt well up her thighs to manoeuvre into place and once she was astride the seat she kept sliding forward towards the depression created by Adam's greater weight. Her thighs scraped against the outside seam of his denims as she positioned her feet and when it came to her hands she was in something of a dilemma.

'I know the advertising claim is that they're rugged enough to tow a car with, but if you hang on to my jeans like that, Honor, they might peel off on a tight curve.'

Honor could feel those tight curves—they were pressed snugly against the V of her legs! She reluctantly let go of his belt loops and tentatively reached around his thick waist, closing her eyes tightly as she felt her hands tangle briefly with the flapping sides of his shirt before connecting with a hard wall of flesh. His skin was hot and slightly moist, so that her palms slid slickly across it. The thicket of hair on his chest, her touch soon discovered, narrowed to a broad streak over his taut belly, springy and vital.

He turned his head, the profile of his lips barely moving as he murmured, 'Hold me harder, Honor, I won't break.'

Honor took a deep breath and leaned further into the convex curve of his back, her breasts flattening against striated muscle, her fingers meshing in a little rush over his navel, catching up a few stray curls as they did so. He made a small, choking sound of mingled pain and laughter that seemed to ripple through every muscle in his body.

'Sorry!'

'Did you do that on purpose?'

'Of course I didn't,' she denied. 'It's not my fault you're hairy.'

'I could shave if you prefer your men smooth.'

As if he cared what she preferred! Although at least he'd paid her the compliment of the plural.

'Shave your chest?' Her mouth suddenly curved as she imagined it. 'Maybe you'd better not,' she said, a bubble of laughter bursting in her throat. 'Your hairiness

might hide a multitude of sins...the way men grow
beards to hide weak chins.'

'I didn't choose to be like this, you know; genetics
decided it for me. It's not a matter of vanity.' Did he
sound slightly piqued?

'Your father, he was a hairy man,' chuckled Honor,
her arms contracting automatically with her mirth.

'He was, as a matter of fact. And he still had a full
head of hair the day he died!'

He really was miffed. Honor muffled her giggles in
the back of his shirt.

'If you can control yourself we'll get started,' he
rumbled sternly, turning the ignition key jerkily and
causing a misfire.

'Yes, Rapunzel, sir,' she said meekly.

His diaphragm tensed under her hand as he twisted
far enough sideways to be able to see her laughter-
contorted face and merry eyes. She tried unsuccessfully
to look serious and a wry half-smile touched his mouth
in response. 'No wonder Sara thinks she's found a
kindred spirit.' His smile deepened. 'You're not really
in an ideal position to provoke me, lady, with your dress
hiked up to your waist and your legs wrapped around
mine.'

'Are you going to start your engine, or just sit here
boasting about it?' Honor countered pertly.

'Feeling your oats, are you, honey?' he rasped, taking
off his hat and stuffing it under his thigh. 'That's good,
because my engine has been revving for the last five
minutes.'

It was a wild ride. After the first few minutes Honor
forgot her modesty and tried to climb inside him as she
hung on over the bumps and hollows. He weaved along
the gravel tractor paths and finally detoured through one
of the kiwi-fruit blocks, Honor instinctively ducking as
they zipped under the leafy, spreading vines trained along
a canopy of wires strung between stout wooden posts.
The vines were supported at a comfortable height for an

average man to stand under without stooping so her unnecessary cringing made Adam laugh, as did her little squeal when he executed a smart one hundred and eighty-degree turn at the end of the row and started back down again. In the end Honor was laughing with him, the wind whipping her hair into a mad froth around her face, the words she tried to shout at him instantly snatched from her mouth and lost in their turbulent wake. It was a long time since Honor had experienced the intoxicating thrill of sheer physical recklessness.

Well, at least all of four days!

When Honor tried to scramble off in the paddock behind the house her legs showed an alarming tendency to fold underneath her.

'You were showing off,' she gasped, as Adam lifted her off in a flurry of gathered skirts and supported her elbows as she found her feet again.

He grinned. 'Just a bit. I made sure to stay out of the blocks that are being worked but I hope we weren't spotted by a rogue crew member. There's a threat of dismissal out on anyone who's caught joy-riding on the farm equipment.'

'They can't fire you, you're the boss.' Honor was still trying to cope with the effect of the exhilaration on her nerves. 'I wonder why they call it *joy*-riding?' she said shakily.

Still holding one of her elbows, Adam waltzed her around her to face him. 'Are you going to tell me you didn't enjoy it?' he teased. 'Come on, Honor, I dare you. Look me dead in the eye and tell me that.'

She felt a tick in the corner of her eye even at the prospect of answering his challenge. He laughed, taking her by the hand and tugging her towards the gate that led to the house like a small boy heading for a treat.

'Why did you come looking for me?' she asked, as they got close enough to see Joy laying out plates on a table in the shadow of a large blue canvas umbrella.

'Mmm?'

'Sara said you were looking for me.'

'Oh, yes, to tell you that the police caught our man. I think I'll have a swim before lunch—going to join me?'

'No, I—*what* did you say?' He had slipped it in so casually, she thought she must have been mistaken.

'I said I think I'll have a——'

'No, I meant about the *man*. What man? You mean the blackmailer? The police have *caught* him?' She stopped in her tracks, jerking him to a halt. 'My God, why didn't you *tell* me?'

'I thought I just did,' he said impatiently.

'I mean straight away! How could you keep it to yourself like that? When did it happen? Who was it? I mean...it's—well, it's terrific...' Her enthusiasm abruptly petered out as her eyes met his and the true impact of what he was saying hit her.

He turned and continued down the path, Honor trotting numbly beside him. 'Actually the police didn't catch him, his wife did. She found the magazines he'd been cutting the letters out of and made him tell her what he'd done. He turned himself in. He'd applied for a job at Blake Investments two years ago but turned up roaring drunk for the interview so the paperwork was never even filed. He hasn't been able to get work since and apparently decided on his last drunken binge that it was time the company paid for causing all his problems. He doesn't admit he's an alcoholic. He didn't really have any plan beyond sending the letters to make us squirm. It was revenge he was after, not the money, so there was no need for him to take the risk of carrying out his threats. He just wanted to "make the bastards suffer".'

He sounded bored. As if now the puzzle was solved he had lost all interest. As if he had weightier matters on his mind.

Honor swallowed. 'What happens now?'

'Now? The police get on with their work and we get back to business as usual.' Was that an oblique hint that Honor also should get back to where she belonged?

'I hope there aren't mushrooms on that pizza, Mum,' he said as they stopped at the table and he reached past his mother for a gently steaming slice.

Joy slapped his hand away. 'Yours is still in the oven. That's for Sara and Honor. It has lots of mushrooms.'

'Why don't you sit down? I'll go in and get it.'

'Sara's fetching it now.' Joy smoothed her bright checked skirt with her hands and took a deep breath. 'I wish you wouldn't treat me like an invalid, Adam. It makes me feel like one. I don't like it.'

He looked startled, then he grinned and leaned into the shade and kissed her wrinkled cheek. 'Has Honor been giving you assertiveness lessons on the sly?'

His mother looked pleased. 'She gave me a book. You don't think I'm going overboard, do you? Your father hated bossy women.'

Adam laughed. 'Don't spoil it now.'

Honor couldn't understand how he could be so casual when she was racked with uncertainty. 'Adam——'

'You may as well sit down and start, since yours is already here. I'll just nip in to change and have a quick dip to loosen up. I've done a couple of hours' hard labour helping with the summer pruning on the kiwi-fruit vines this morning and I'm beginning to feel a few muscles I didn't know I had.'

'Adam, I need to talk to you...'

'Later, hmm?' He was stripping of his shirt and Honor couldn't help noticing the row of eight small, crescent-shaped indentations in the vicinity of his navel. Goodness, she hadn't realised she'd dug her fingernails in that hard. Out of the corner of her eye she saw Joy look at her son and rushed into speech.

'No, now. It's about my leaving. Now this thing's wrapped up surely there's no danger, no need——'

He grabbed her jaw and stopped her saying any more by the simple expedient of kissing her.

'There's always a need. You're my means, remember?' He rubbed his hard nose against hers as he lifted his mouth. 'You have a job you haven't finished yet; you can't leave until that's done. And I still haven't got around to returning those letters of yours, have I? You certainly can't leave until you have those in your hot little hand...'

CHAPTER EIGHT

HONOR knelt back on her heels and sighed with frustration. The bottom drawer of the walnut desk was locked. She had jiggled experimentally at the handle but there was no way that it was going to fly open 'accidentally' and reveal its contents.

Light from the lamp on the desk glinted off a letter-opener lying beside it and she was tempted to try jabbing the point into the keyhole, but the temptation was only fleeting. The art of jimmying locks was not in her repertoire of skills and even if she flunked it there was a very definite line between surreptitiously searching and outright breaking and entering. It would be a gross abuse of hospitality, not to mention reprehensible criminal behaviour. Honor might be desperate but she wasn't yet a complete moral degenerate.

She sighed again and put her hands flat on the carpet to lever herself to her feet.

'Lost a contact lens?'

Her head snapped up so violently at the sarcastic enquiry that it collided with the overhanging corner of the desk.

'Ouch!' She rose, rubbing the sore spot, pain taking the edge off her shock at the sight of the big man who had flicked on the overhead light.

There was something not quite right about him in the stark elegance of a dinner suit, she thought dizzily. He looked magnificent, but rigid and uncomfortably formal.

She wondered if he had looked so cool and austere on the night of the Valentine's Ball. Probably. She had learned from Joy, after some judicious prompting, that he had gone that night in a threesome with Zach and Tania in the latter's brand-new Holden Commodore—Helen's contemptible US-influenced 'station wagon or something'—with some reluctance.

Mary had been born on the fifteenth of February and he was always a bit broody and melancholy on the eve of her birthday anniversary, Joy had confided, and his family had thought the distraction would be good for him. In his vulnerable state it wasn't surprising that he had been a sucker for a damsel in distress, Honor had thought gloomily, especially if Helen reminded him of his beautiful wife. He himself had confessed that sending the valentine card the next day had been pure impulse, intended merely as a whimsical passing tribute to an intriguing beauty, and the swift, entertaining reply had taken him by surprise.

'You're back!' she blurted inanely. She had watched his Mercedes roll out of the drive not twenty minutes ago, heading for a business function in Auckland. Even as the tail-lights disappeared into the fine mist of evening drizzle she had been busy planning how to take full advantage of his unexpected absence.

Honor watched him carefully close the door by leaning back against it.

'Not before time, it would seem,' he said silkily. 'You've obviously lost something of value. Or should I say—failed to find it?' His gaze went thoughtfully over her black muslin draw-string skirt and matching crop-top. 'Are you dressed that way for dinner, or for cat-burglary? Basic black is so versatile that way, don't you think?'

'I thought you were going to be away for hours—you said you might even stay in town overnight.' Honor glared at him, as if he were the one who had been caught red-handed.

'I had a flat just down the hill, at the turn-off for the Scenic Drive.' He brushed at his shoulders, drawing her attention to the glittering sheen of dampness on the fine black fabric and the speckles of mud ringing the lower edges of his trousers. 'Since I was going to get wet and dirty whatever I did, it seemed quicker to leave the Merc and come back for a change of clothes and another car. But perhaps now I won't go at all. Not when the prospect of a *far* more interesting evening has come up...'

She couldn't mistake what he meant as he moved—no, *prowled* away from the door into the room, the unfamiliar stiffness melting into something more provocatively familiar as he flicked open the black tie and unbuttoned the high collar of his white shirt with a sigh of pleasurable relief.

He shrugged out of his jacket and tossed it with typical careless disregard for its expensive tailoring across the back of the small two-seater couch opposite the wall of bookshelves. Still in leisurely motion, he skirted behind his desk, reaching into his deep pocket to draw out a set of keys, the smallest of which he used to unlock the drawer that had given her so much frustration. He opened it with a small, theatrical flourish and stood back with an inviting flip of his hand that invited her to investigate.

She didn't even bother to look down, her attention riveted by the liquid gleam in his eyes and the dangerous sweetness of his smile. Her head throbbed and her heart fluttered. It wasn't his anger she had to fear...

'Not interested? There are some papers in there containing commercially sensitive information that certain people would pay you well for. And there's my safe— have you tried that yet?' He waved towards the wall.

His sarcasm had its usual bracing effect. 'You know very well I'm not an industrial spy,' she said truculently. 'I just want what's rightfully mine...'

And that includes you. Honor pressed her hand over her mouth, horrified that the careless words might actually have slipped out.

They hadn't. Adam continued to look at her with that seductive mockery.

'Poor Honor, you really are tied up in knots about those letters, aren't you?' he said gravely. 'Here, let me look at that bump.'

Only he didn't just look at it. His hand winnowed through her curls to hold her head still while the fingers of his other hand gently sought the stinging bruise.

She shied away when he touched it, conscious of the mingled scent of damp fabric and musky male sweat that rose from the heat of his body.

'Adam——'

'Shh, hold still. Mmm. I don't think you're in any danger of complications. I know what'll make you feel better——'

Honor closed her eyes and inhaled deeply. Yes, so do I—you! she replied silently.

'The same as I do—a good, stiff drink,' he said disappointingly. 'Come and sit down; it's about time we had a serious talk about something that might change your mind about continuing your criminal career.'

With those ominous words he led her, unresisting, over to the couch and pressed her down into the soft cushions, leaving her there while he slid back a panel in the bookcase, revealing an array of bottles and a mini-fridge. Honor was chagrined to realise that she hadn't even discovered that innocuous little hiding place during her hasty, intermittent searches. Some criminal mastermind *she* would make!

He poured himself a large whisky on the rocks and added ginger ale to her small one, by now accustomed to her preferences.

'Now——' He sat down beside her and waited until she took a sip, turning his glass slowly between his hands as he said slowly, 'I have a confession to make——'

Honor didn't let him finish. 'I knew it! You don't have them. You've already thrown them away!' she interrupted bleakly. Suddenly it didn't seem the most favourable of the worst-case scenarios she had lined up after all.

That day beside the pool she had been so grateful of any excuse to stay that she had meekly let Adam think that he had threatened her into submission, but in the magic week that followed she had had time to regret her weakness. Did he still have those letters or didn't he? Was he a control freak or an opportunist? In the end she had taken matters into her own hands and begun her surreptitious quest.

Meanwhile, although she had continued to perform all her regular work without hindrance, somehow something was always coming up to stop her from completing the Blake pamphlet...usually Adam himself. He was working in his own office downstairs but he seemed to have a sixth sense operating, for whenever she got to the point of calling up his file on her computer with the intent of fixing the final layout he would arrive with additional inclusions that necessitated editing or rewriting several other passages.

He had also insisted that in order to be fully involved in the project she had to know the people and places she was writing for and about. Nearly every day he whisked her away for a few hours to explore some interesting new corner of the sprawling Blake empire, providing her in the process with her first true inkling of what an important man he was, and the incredible weight of responsibility he now bore on his broad shoulders.

Often they had Sara chatting along in tow, a slyly observant chaperon, apparently perfectly happy but still rigidly avoiding the subject of school. Adam had gone into Auckland one day to see the headmistress, gaining her agreement to keep Sara at home a bit longer as long as she undertook to do several hours' set schoolwork a day. He had taken Honor with him, dropping her at a

radio station in the morning where she'd spent the day
recording a new set of station promos.

'If you knew I didn't have them, why were you
searching my office?' Adam asked with impeccable logic.

She took another hurried sip, then a full-throated
swallow. It lubricated her thoughts considerably and
warmed her hollow stomach.

'I thought you might have just misplaced them. You
have an awful lot of paperwork floating around here,
and I thought if I had a look around...' She drank
thirstily. It gave her something to do with her hands and
her flapping mouth. Why didn't he help her? This was
supposed to be *his* confession! 'Do you think I could
have another of these?'

Adam looked down at his full glass, then put it down
and silently got up to fetch her another one, a little larger
than the first.

'You should have just told me,' she continued as he
came back beside her. 'I would have understood. I mean,
I wouldn't have been offended or anything. I realise you
must have found them hideously embarrassing——'

'Must I?'

His quiet tone soothed her fears. 'I mean, let's face
it, we all do things that we later regret. I don't want you
to think that I thought *you* thought I would take you
seriously...' She frowned as she heard how complicated
that sounded. Was that what she had meant to say? She
didn't know, so she decided to put it another way. 'Not
that I have men writing me passionate love-letters so
often I'm blasé about it or anything, but you have to
take that kind of thing with a grain of salt if you're
sensible...'

'And you're very sensible.'

She was glad he understood that. 'Yes.'

'So sensible that you wrote back and told me very
sensibly to stop writing such nonsense to you.'

Honor went scarlet and choked on the dregs of her whisky. He obligingly thumped her back until she got herself under control. By then her eyes were streaming.

He took a slightly limp, rain-spotted handkerchief out of his trouser pocket and she scrubbed her eyes with it fiercely, glad she hadn't got around to putting on her make-up. Dining with Tania was always a case of Full War-Paint Will Be Worn. At least having a model as an elder sister had meant she could hold her own in the skill of application, even if she didn't have the other woman's prime raw material to work with.

'You know very well——'

'Ah, but that's the catch. I don't. You see, I've never written any passionate love-letters to you, so how could I have received replies to them? The only correspondence I've ever had with *you* are those amiable and argumentative, touching and funny letters we exchange once a month——'

'But that's impossible—they were in your handwriting—they were addressed to me—that is, to Helen—but they came to *me!*' She was shocked by his absurd attempt to deny what they both knew were the facts. *This* was his grand confession?

'But not *hand*-addressed. The envelopes were computer printed, weren't they? Because after the first few letters I formatted your address-label into my word-processing files.'

'But the letters——'

'Oh, the *letters* were mine, I admit that. But they weren't *yours*. They were never meant for you...or for your sister. The only love-letters I've ever written in my life were sent years and years ago, when I was still in my impetuous youth, to a sweetheart I was head over heels in love with...'

'I...I don't understand.' The whiskey fumes that had gone to her head were dispelled by a cold chill. She was very much afraid that she *was* beginning to understand what he was trying, very gently, to break to her.

Another Helen? Not Helen Sheldon? Not her sister?

The magnitude of his revelation hit Honor like an avalanche.

My God, there was yet another gorgeous woman haunting his past! She couldn't imagine him being un-faithful to his flawless Mary so that meant that Helen must have pre-dated her, a young man's first dream of passion where Mary had been the paragon of his maturity.

And every 'darling', every 'sweeting', every romantic word of Shakespeare and John Donne...'If ever any beauty I did see, Which I desir'd, and got, t'was but a dreame of thee'... every dear, delicious loop and curl of every exquisite, erotic word that Honor had treasured was so much meaningless gibberish! It wasn't the shining beauty of her inner soul revealed to him on paper that had seduced him into his intense love-affair with words, it was the ghostly image of a former lover preserved!

Honor winced. One paragon to contend with had been depressing enough to contend with...but *two*? At least she no longer had to worry about her sister being a rival. Adam was not one to pine helplessly over lost oppor-tunities. If he had really wanted to contact Helen he would have had no hesitation in asking Honor for her address!

'Oh, Honor, there's really no delicate way of telling you this, is there?' he said, taking a brooding slug of his own drink before continuing bluntly, 'As far as I know, those old letters were up in one of the attics here somewhere, in a suitcase along with a lot of my other happy memories.' He looked down at her fist, white knuckles clenched around his monogrammed handker-chief. 'She made a point of giving them back to me, you see...so I would never be able to forget what it had felt like to first fall in love. As if I would or could! Anyway, they...well, you can understand what they meant to me...they were a very precious part of my personal history.'

Oh, yes, Honor could understand all right. She knew *exactly* what it meant to cherish a dream.

'When Malcolm told me you were cleared and showed me the letter he'd taken off you, I couldn't believe it! I rushed back here and hunted through the attic like a wild man, and when I couldn't find them—well, I can't describe how I felt. That's why I burst in on you like Attila the Hun. If you had them then for my own peace of mind you *had* to be guilty of something...*anything*! But, instead of getting answers, all I found were more questions. You didn't have all the letters for a start. And, in case you didn't notice, almost all those you were sent seemed carefully selected to preserve a kind of anonymity on both sides—no names or addresses...'

'Oh, I noticed all right...too late,' said Honor grimly.

'It was just a wretchedly unfortunate coincidence that it came to a head at the same time as this other thing.' Adam tipped her chin with his hand, forcing her to meet his earnest gaze. 'You can see that I had to keep you here, can't you? I had to find out if you had the others, if it was just a silly charade or a conspiracy...'

Honor jerked her head away from his touch. 'Well, it wasn't!'

'I realised that in fairly short order,' he said wryly. 'But that only made things worse as far as I was concerned. It meant I had to look closer to home for the culprit. Reasoning it out from the postal dates on the envelopes, the first switch occurred not long after I moved in here, after Zach's death. It had to be someone who had access to the attic and the opportunity to pull the necessary switches—lift my regular outgoing correspondence to you and substitute the fake letters. Not only that, but they would have to intercept your replies, otherwise I would realise something was going on.'

Honor blanched at the thought of her love lying bleeding in the hands of some psychologically disturbed individual. But not a stranger. This was nothing to do with Adam's company, this was very, very personal. Therefore it stood to reason that it had to be someone personally very close to Adam. That was the reason for his solemn calm.

'But what possibly could be the motive?' she cried, not wanting to believe that anyone he trusted could betray him so viciously. 'A practical joke? Surely not? Who would want to be so unbearably cruel...not just to me but to you?'

Adam remained silent, watching her as she groped towards the consciousness of what he had already guessed.

Honor could only think of one person who resented her badly enough to want to hurt her.

'I don't...surely *Tania* wouldn't——?'

'Tania?' Adam shook his head. 'I wouldn't put it past her deliberately to cause a few letters to go astray if it suited her purposes, but go to all that trouble to generate a potentially violent awareness between us? I think not.' Adam's hand slid over both of hers, trapping their restless mangling of his handkerchief. 'If she wanted to throw a spanner into our relationship, why would she make a meeting between us inevitable by encouraging you to believe that I was in love with you? I presume in your letters you referred to mine?' She nodded, colour returning in a rush to her cheeks, and he studied her with glinting satisfaction. 'That's why I wasn't allowed to receive any replies. It would have given the game away too soon. You needed to be convinced first...'

'But *why*?' Honor still couldn't conceive of a motive for a plan of such pointless complexity.

'Perhaps for the best reason in the world. Love.'

'*Love*?' Honor's exclamation made it sound as if she'd never even heard of the word.

He smiled crookedly at her confusion. 'Perhaps someone who loved me was worried about me. Maybe they thought that I was urgently in need of a love-life—even if it was of the mail-order kind—to rescue me from emotional limbo.'

Honor sucked in a startled breath. 'Your *mother* . . . ?'

'I think it's the most likely possibility, don't you think?'

She remembered the way that Joy had welcomed her into the house, declaring that she knew how special she was to Adam.

'Have you asked her?'

'Not outright, no.' His smile took a downward trend as he admitted ruefully, 'It's a pretty tough assignment—accusing your own mother of theft and forgery when you don't have a shred of proof. If I'm wrong she could be terribly hurt. And if I'm right...well, I was worried that it might mean Mum is getting as bad as Tania's been suggesting.' He stroked his thumb absently over her knuckles as he chuckled. 'But then I realised the opposite was true; no one in a state of mental confusion could possibly have succeeded in carrying out such a complicated, machiavellian scheme. Hell, I doubt even I would have been able to pull it off half so well!'

'I think you're actually proud of her,' Honor murmured wryly. It was fine for him, but she was in a far less enviable position. 'I don't care about where the rest of *your* letters are, but what has she done with mine?'

'Ah, yes, the sober, sensible replies to my intoxicated ramblings.' He slid his arm along the back of the couch, dislodging his damp jacket, his other hand covering both of hers as he leaned teasingly towards her. 'What will you give me if I promise to get them back for you?'

'I don't have to give you anything,' she said breathlessly as he loomed closer. 'You've already promised to give them to me, with no strings attached.'

'Oh, yes.' His eyes sank to her parted lips. 'That night when you flirted into my bedroom in your silky, see-through nightshirt...'

'I didn't flirt... and it wasn't see-through,' she said weakly, leaning further and further back as his mouth leisurely approached. He was going to kiss her and there wasn't a thing she could do about it—unless she got up and left the room, of course...

'Enticed, then... and that's funny, because when I'm alone at night, tossing and turning in my lovely bed, I'm haunted by this vivid memory of your breasts in my hands and my mouth——'

'Are you trying to make me feel sorry for you?' Honor interrupted tremulously, stunned by the image of him lying in his bed on the other side of the wall, aching for her as she had lain aching for him.

'Is it working?' He brushed his mouth against hers at last.

'No,' she sighed, her whole body going boneless as his mouth brushed again, and settled...

'Hard-hearted witch...' He tasted strongly of whisky, and Honor was quickly over the legal limit, struggling to remember all the reasons why she shouldn't be making it easy for him.

'Adam... the car—your dinner——' she said, arching her throat under his marauding mouth.

'Damn them all,' he rumbled. 'This is more important. I'd rather be doing this right now than anything in the world...' He pushed her deeper into the cushions, aligning his body over hers, as he slid one side of her blouse down and nuzzled her bare shoulder. 'Why don't we go somewhere where we can be alone?'

'We are alone.'

'Not enough. I mean really alone. This is one aspect of my love-life where I definitely don't need any assistance. I think I remember all the right moves...'

He certainly did, Honor thought hazily, loving the warmth and weight of him, the beat of his heart setting a new rhythm for her blood. What a pity he didn't remember the right words to go with them.

'What do you expect from me, Adam?' she whispered pleadingly.

He kissed the corner of her mouth and stroked the tip of his tongue briefly into the silky crevice. 'You have to ask?' His amusement shimmered with masculine awareness.

'Yes,' she said threadily. 'I think I do.'

His expression of heavy-lidded sensuality changed subtly as he shifted sideways, raising himself on one elbow, his hand moving with slow deliberation from her waist to just below her breasts where it spanned her ribcage. The anticipation of his touch was almost unbearable as he murmured, 'You do?'

She nodded, barely, as his mouth lowered to graze the upper curve of her breast, exposed by the sideways slide of her black top.

'Are you sure about that, darling?' His breath crept under the neckline in a moist and secret caress and she shut her eyes as she felt her breasts tauten. He knew she was sensitive there. He knew all her secrets...except one.

She shivered and found that she couldn't answer. Why did he have to ask? He must know the reassurance she needed. Why couldn't he just *lie*, and allow them both the luxury of pretending to believe it?

'Honor?'

She opened her eyes and could have wept. An expression of gritty determination was layered over the silky hot, sensual need that had been flaring out of control moments ago. For the first time she hated him for his magnificent strength of character.

'I'm selfish,' he said huskily. 'And greedy. I don't want to lose a friend to gain a lover. I want both.' He rolled off the couch to stand up in one fluid motion, pulling her with him and holding her hard against him for a single, searing instant before thrusting her away.

'You asked what do I expect from you? The answer is nothing but what you're prepared to give,' he said, safe behind the barrier of his tightly leashed control. 'So how about giving me some honesty? For instance—why don't you tell me how it made you feel to open a letter and find out that I was suddenly headlong in love with you? Shocked? Disgusted? Amused? And tell me how you felt when you finally realised that I thought you were somebody else. Not what you did—what you *felt*!'

She had put her feelings for him into words once and it had all gone horribly wrong. She had learned a bitter lesson from her mistake.

'I felt—amused,' she said with cracked defiance, opening her eyes as wide as possible, so that they stung with the effort, and even managing a little trill of a laugh. 'It was so much like a French farce: turgid over-emotionalism and mislaid messages and mistaken identities, ridiculous entrances and exits. To have taken it seriously would have been plain stupid!'

'So you find it all rather amusing?' His voice sounded thick with uncertainty and she nearly relented. But then she remembered how little he had told her about *his* feelings.

She lifted her head. 'Yes.'

His eyes were pale with a savage triumph. 'Then why are you crying?'

Her hand flew to her cheek and she was aghast to find it was true. This fresh self-betrayal by her body was the last straw.

'Because I hate you, that's why!' she screamed hysterically, vainly trying to wipe away the humiliating evidence only to find she was using the handkerchief he had given her. She flung it at his head and rushed past him to fling open the door.

Standing on the other side, her hand raised to knock timidly, was Sara, neatly dressed for dinner in one of her aunt's sedate choices.

'Oh!' Honor was still trying to stem the ceaseless tide. She knew she must look red-nosed and swollen-eyed and hideous. That must be why Sara was screwing up her face. She cast an agonised look over her shoulder at Adam and in that instant Sara gave a little sobbing gasp.

'I'm sorry. I'm so sorry.' Like a rocket the girl was gone, sturdy legs pumping as she pounded up the stairs. Honor was riveted in shock as Adam brushed roughly past her.

She caught his arm, instinctively driven to try to help. 'Adam——'

He turned on her abruptly. 'Let me go to her. For God's sake, haven't you already done enough damage tonight?'

His accusation was so unfair it took her breath away. It wasn't her fault that Sara might have overheard their argument, even though it was Honor who had been doing the shouting. Whatever else he thought about her, he must know she wouldn't deliberately involve a child in an adult conflict.

It was a miserable dinner. Neither Adam nor Sara appeared and Joy had obviously decided the time was ripe to practise her assertiveness on Tania. She announced over the cold soup that she had enrolled in Indian-cooking classes run by the wife of a local accountant who commuted to work in the city. She only had to wait a bare instant for the expected response.

'At your age?' Tania frowned her doubting disapproval. 'You'd probably only get in the way of the other students. And think of all that standing. Why don't you go down to the hobby shop at Evansdale if you want something to do? They have some lovely tapestry canvases for sale.'

'I don't like sewing. I prefer cooking.' Joy had marshalled her logic expertly. 'And Adam agrees that I'm quite well enough to do as much of it as I like. Rhonda told me she'd be glad to be back to her old eight-to-four routine again.'

'I don't know why you want to learn to cook curries; you know I don't like spicy foods——'

'But you're here so rarely for dinner these days, my dear. And Indian cooking isn't only curries. There's a vast array of regional dishes——'

And so it went on, back and forth, while Honor's attention remained tuned to the silent upper floors.

At last, when she could stand it no longer, she excused herself and took her cup of coffee up to her office but after half an hour of trying to proofread the annual report of a local community service organisation she gave up in disgust. Proofreading required strict concentration and meticulous attention to detail and she just wasn't in the right frame of mind. Once or twice she heard a heavy tread along the hall but her desk was at the wrong angle to catch anything more than a brief glimpse of movement past the half-open door. No one sought her out. Even Monty had abandoned her for the pleasures of roaming his new domain, having established complete domination of the existing local feline population with his usual brawling finesse.

Finally she could stand the suspense no longer.

Her feet carried her past Adam's firmly closed bedroom door, from behind which came the faint sound of the FM Concert Programme to which his radio was permanently tuned, to the one that bore a ceramic rosebud plaque with 'Sara' inexpertly engraved on it, product of a school art-class project, Honor had been proudly informed.

With a nervous look along the hall Honor pressed her ear to the wood above the plaque. Prying, lying, eavesdropping...what miserable depths would she sink to next?

When she heard no murmur of voices within and knew it was safe to assume that Adam was elsewhere, she knocked softly.

A very subdued Sara was sitting at her dressing-table staring glumly into the mirror. The dress she had been wearing had been exchanged for the racy-looking, parachute-silk tracksuit that Honor had impulsively bought for her one day, when a tour with Adam had happened to end up next door to a childrenswear factory-shop.

'Daddy said I have to apologise.' The girl sighed, moving over to sit cross-legged on the rose-coloured bedspread. 'I was just practising.'

'I think that sort of thing is better *not* practised,' Honor told her wryly, feeling some of her tension relax. The tracksuit was a good sign. 'Spontaneity is usually best if you want to sound sincere. Anyway, I should be the one saying I'm sorry. I didn't mean to upset you downstairs. Your father and I were—uh—talking and I lost my temper.'

'You said you hated him. He made you cry,' Sara pointed out flatly.

'That was temper talking and he didn't *make* me cry, I managed that all by myself,' Honor admitted. 'I get emotional sometimes.'

'PMT,' Sara nodded sagely. 'I don't have to worry about that yet.'

She grinned suddenly, her slightly pink eyes creasing up the way her father's did when he was going to deliver a particularly stunning piece of mockery. 'I just get PT— *Pre-adolescent* Tension.'

Honor had to swallow a laugh, feeling they were in severe danger of losing track of the conversation. 'What did your dad think you had to apologise about?' she said hurriedly.

'Oh, w-e-l-l...' Sara drew in a long, deep breath as she put off the evil moment. She picked up one of her pillows and hugged it to her flat chest. Her chin took on a square, pugnacious aspect. 'It was me!'

'You who?' responded Honor blankly. Luckily Sara didn't respond with her usual swiftness to the verbal absurdity.

'Who sent you those letters that Dad wrote. You know, the mushy ones.' She watched Honor's face sag, her body following as she sank down on the bed beside the incredible child.

'Dad said you'd be upset. I didn't do it to hurt anyone—— '

'I know you didn't,' responded Honor automatically, still trying to adjust to the idea of a pint-sized Machiavelli instead of an elderly one.

'It was just that I didn't want Dad to marry Aunt Tania.'

'*Marry* her?' Honor felt sick at the idea. 'Whatever made you think he was going to?'

Sara hugged her cushion tighter and said defensively, 'You don't know what it was like. After we moved in here she was always hanging around Dad, sucking up to him, making stupid sheep's-eyes at him and telling him how much she needed him. It was gross!

'Not that he's dumb or anything but Dad's at a dangerous age, you know. He'll be forty in a few years and I thought he might marry Aunt Tania in a panic about getting old and decrepit and his manhood withering away...' Sara described her father's imagined decline with vivid enthusiasm.

'You see, since Mum died he's spent most of his spare time doing things with me—he's afraid I'll get emotionally deprived or something. I mean, at least I go to parties and stuff with my friends but Dad would rather read a book or listen to music for fun, so what chance is there for him to meet anyone else? Aunt Tania tries to hog all his attention. She even nagged him into taking her to the business things that his secretary used to be his hostess for, and called them dates. Yuk!

'I suppose she was OK when she was just my aunt and we didn't see her that often but I couldn't hack her as a stepmother. She's always wanting to change me, and Dad too, and sometimes he lets her get away with things because he couldn't be bothered arguing with her.'

She took a deep breath. 'Then I remembered about you. Whenever a letter arrived with your handwriting on it Dad would get a big grin on his face, even if he was tired and grouchy. He read the good bits out to me sometimes and I thought that you sounded really funny. Clever, too, not like Aunt Tania who doesn't get half of his jokes! Dad said you were just pen-friends and I thought that meant you lived too far away but I snooped around one day and found out your address. I thought he might be afraid of meeting you in case you didn't like him in person or that he knew you were real shy or something. He had this newspaper photograph of you, too, in his top drawer—well, it wasn't you, was it? I guess it was your sister—in this white glittery dress at the Valentine's Ball and you—*she* looked really happy and smiley and *much* more beautiful than Aunt Tania.

'So when I was playing up in the attic one day and found those old letters of Dad's I thought *you* might ask to meet *him* if you found out what a terrific, sexy guy he could be. He's real romantic, don't you think, to be able to write awesome letters like that...?' She sighed mistily and paused for an unusual moment of silent contemplation. 'So I picked some that didn't have any dates or anything on them and were all just, you know, the hot stuff...' She grimaced. 'I guess it was pretty rotten of me, huh? Like Dad taking my ultra-secret diary and letting someone else read it—that's what he said.

'Anyway, in the end it all went much easier than I thought because since he's been here Dad always leaves his personal letters on the hall table for Rhonda to post on her way home from work and all the mail he has redirected from his post-office box gets left there, too. Only nothing seemed to happen for ages and Aunt Tania started hinting to me that wouldn't it be nice to have a mother to share things with, so then I was desperate and got myself suspended so that Dad wouldn't be alone around here with her so much—you know, in case she got him in a weak moment...' She looked at Honor sheepishly. 'Only you arrived on the same day, and...'

'And I wasn't the beautiful fairy princess you were expecting,' Honor finished her sentence ruefully.

'No, but you turned out to be OK,' Sara said offhandedly magnanimous. 'You sure put Aunt Tania's nose out of joint!' She discarded her pillow and flopped across the bed with a frown. 'Except I didn't really help, did I? Because none of it was real. Dad said you can't *make* people love each other, however many tricks you play on them. In the end it's up to them.

'But I want you to know, Honor, that I never read any of the letters you sent back—at least, not after I looked at the first one to make sure you weren't terminally grossed-out or anything,' she corrected herself earnestly. 'I didn't even open the envelopes. I didn't really know what to do with them so I just put them straight in the cardboard box I sellotaped under my chest of drawers—where I keep my diary. Aunt Tania snoops too, you see. Dad says as a family we have no respect for privacy.'

'Perhaps you might see your way clear to letting me have them back, then,' said Honor gravely.

'Oh, sure. But you'll have to ask Dad. He took them after we had our talk. I have to go back to school on Monday and stay in my room for—— Hey, Honor, where are you going?'

*   *   *

Like his daughter, Adam was lying on his back on his bed, with one significant difference: he was surrounded by carelessly torn-open envelopes and numerous lined sheets of delicate blue writing paper. He was reading intently. Good God, she had even perfumed the things with a sprinkle of dried flowers from her garden!

'How dare you? You thieving, rotten, unconscionable pig! Give those back to me!' she gasped as she burst into the room and launched herself without hesitation across him, grabbing madly at the pieces of paper that swished and swirled around them in a sea of giant blue confetti, stuffing pages down the neck of her blouse as fast as she could, trying to avoid Adam's laughing attempts to retrieve them.

'What's the matter, Honor? You're so serious,' he taunted when she swore bitterly at the discovery that her black top wouldn't accept any more stuffing without bursting its buttons. 'Isn't this funny? Isn't this a farce?' He caught her around the waist, her chest crackling furiously as he pulled her down and declared in a furious hiss, 'Don't ever lie to me like that again! My God, I was right when I said you were gullible, wasn't I? A reckless, hot-headed, gullible romantic! You fell for it like a ton of bricks. Didn't it *occur* to you to check up on me first? That writing things like this to a man you'd never met was a bloody dangerous thing to do? What if I had turned out to be some psychotic sex maniac looking for my next victim?'

'You might yet!' she spat back, flushed with fury and embarrassment and the strange, shocking novelty of having a hundred and fifty pounds of angry male thrust vibrating beneath her.

'You're going to have ample opportunity to find out!' he vowed, the yellow fire in his eyes melting into a savage satisfaction as she continued to scrabble and squirm desperately for the few remaining sheets that weren't crushed under his body. 'I wouldn't bother if I were you, darling. It's too late. I've been reading them for the last half-hour and I have a photographic memory for print. I'm word-perfect already... care to test me?'

'You——'

Her lips were sealed by a calloused finger. 'Now calm down and I'll help you to collect them up. What's done is done, Honor. Now there's nothing left for you to hide. Learn to live with it.' His deceptively calm voice lowered to a silken murmur that shook her from the boughs of her anger. 'My belated thanks for the lovely compliments, by the way. No one has ever written to me in quite such uninhibited terms before...'

'What about your original Helen?' Honor retorted, easing herself away, determined that he would never be able to call her gullible again. To her surprise he let her go.

'My Helen of Troy?' He smiled, but it was a smile of amusement rather than remembered passion. 'She wasn't much for expressing herself in words. I left my letters in the proverbial hole in the tree and her replies were usually a matter of a few lines to tell me where and when to meet her. We were star-crossed lovers, you see, and the illicit nature of it made it all that much more exciting.'

Honor compressed her mouth. 'Could you roll over, please? I want to get this last one underneath you.'

'Certainly. Oh, that's my favourite,' he said, peeking. 'Isn't that the one where you said I was——?'

She crushed it to her misshapen chest. '*Goodnight*, Adam,' she said firmly, stepping away from the dangerous territory of his bed.

He stood up and stretched, as contented as a well-fed cat. 'And sweet dreams to you, darling. I certainly know *I'll* have them...'

He walked her to the door, her dignity suffering badly from the loud rustle she emitted with every step. Once there she waited stiffly while he opened it. But before he let her make her escape he caught her back and kissed her, briefly and hard, a promise rather than a threat, his hands running possessively down the whole length of her spine and back up to knead the tension from her shoulders as he told her soothingly, 'Everything'll be fine in the morning, you'll see. A good sleep will put all this in its proper perspective. There'll be no more nasty surprises and awkward complications to get in our way. From now on we can just concentrate on you and me...'

He couldn't have been more wrong!

Next morning, passing through the hall on her way to an early breakfast, alive with feverish anticipation of the promised new day, Honor stopped to answer the front door.

Outside stood a major new delivery of worry and complication, parcelled up in the most exquisite wrapping.

'Surprise!' her sister carolled, dropping her hat-box and spreading her arms in a parody of the welcome that wasn't forthcoming.

'Honor, you naughty thing, you didn't tell me you'd been temporarily elevated to the landed gentry. I had to find out all on my own. Aren't you going to invite me in to meet your generous penfriend?'

CHAPTER NINE

IF HONOR'S arrival had caused surprise, Helen's created a sensation.

Tania, who might have been expected to feel pique at the eclipse of her own beauty by a more celestial body, instead was positively gushing, showing no sign of the hostility that she directed at Honor.

And Joy, typically, was delighted. Of *course* Honor's sister was welcome and of *course* the unusualness of the hour didn't matter—country people were always up early; in fact, wasn't it silly for Helen to go back to Kowhai Hill when her sister was staying right here? Why didn't Helen stay, too?

Honor watched as Helen accepted prettily.

'How convenient that you just *happened* to bring your luggage along with you,' she murmured ironically.

There was no point in trying to whisk Helen quietly away now. The damage had been done the moment Adam stepped out of the dining-room to see what was causing the commotion in the hall. He had looked stunned, then an expression of unholy delight had crossed his face and he had almost tripped over himself in his rush to draw her inside.

Helen gave her one of her famous cool looks. 'I'm a seasoned traveller, darling, I'm always prepared for contingencies. I didn't know what your plans were and I'd rather be at a civilised hotel than that spooky little house in the middle of nowhere if I'm going to be alone.'

Even Sara seemed to have abandoned her usual insouciance, regarding Helen with an awed fascination that was uncomfortably like her father's. Maybe she was thinking that Helen would be better competition for Tania after all, thought Honor ruefully.

Ten minutes after she had arrived Helen was sitting at the head of the family breakfast-table, drinking black coffee and daintily eating fingers of dry toast, regaling the household with the amusing story of how she had tracked Honor down. After letting herself in at Kowhai Hill with the key from under the flower-pot the previous day she had waited all night for Honor to turn up.

'I was beginning to think that my sensible, level-headed sister had finally decided to kick over the traces when who should turn up on my doorstep this morning but the local constable! Some old duck had reported seeing activity in the house when everyone knew that Honor was away.

'I think the poor policeman nearly had a heart attack when I answered the door.' Helen sent a coyly smouldering look towards the man of the house, as if inviting him to imagine the next bit himself. 'I'd been in the shower, you see, and I was only wearing a wrap...'

Adam smiled and responded obligingly.

'I'll bet he did,' he murmured, his warm brown eyes appreciating the view of a filmy white blouse that was almost, but not quite, transparent under her linen jacket.

Helen laughed huskily, pleased. 'When he finally calmed down, the dear man offered to bring me over in his patrol car. Wasn't that sweet of him?'

'You could have telephoned first,' suggested Honor drily, knowing full well that it was blatant curiosity, not concern, that had brought her sister rushing over to visit.

Helen was too busy smiling back at Adam, her almond eyes veiled with the look of seductive mystery that had graced a thousand billboards, to worry about the possible inconsistencies in her story.

'Then it wouldn't have been a surprise. Anyway, on the way over, Mr Plod told me all about that awful man

demanding money with menaces and how Honor wrote
it up for the newspapers.'

Helen managed to drag her attention off Adam long
enough to give her sister some praise.

'How terribly clever of you, sweetie, to turn what
must've been a *ghastly* experience for everyone into such
an advantage.'

Honor smiled weakly. The compliment was not only
dubious, it was also thoroughly undeserved. She could
hardly admit that she had been drifting about in such a
haze that she had forgotten all about her supposedly
ruthless ambition until Adam had jogged her memory
later on the day that he told her about the arrest by telling
her he had arranged for Detective Inspector Marshall to
grant her a joint interview with himself that very evening.
Honor had tried to pretend airily that he had merely pre-
empted her own imminent actions but she had the feeling
that Adam had known damned well that it had all been
bluff.

The rest of the Press had had to wait until the next
afternoon, when the disturbed man had appeared briefly
in court to be remanded in custody for a psychiatric
report, before they got their first official police statement,
and by that time Honor was ringing papers up and down
the country offering to fax them her backgrounder. It
had been snapped up and syndication overseas had nicely
plumped her bank balance, to the extent that she had
rung the garage and told the long-suffering mechanic
that she could now afford to have her VW back. It was
sitting in the drive right now, beside Adam's Mercedes.

'So... you stayed with Honor a fortnight ago, didn't
you?' Adam was saying innocently. 'She didn't tell me
you were expected back again so *soon*...'

Honor felt her neck prickle at the subtly accusing
undertone in his remark but her sister quickly let her
off the hook.

'That's because I wasn't. It was impulse, really, because we were shooting up at the Barrier Reef when this cyclone started looming up on the weather map so we picked up the pace and finished the assignment three days early. I thought, Why not pop in on my way back to New York?

'I'm afraid I had to rush away last time, you see, just when Honor was getting all hyped up about that silly St Valentine's thing, and I must admit I felt a *teeny* bit guilty about not having been more sympathetic and helpful...'

'What St Valentine's thing?' asked Tania, perking up with interest in something other than the attire and exciting lifestyle of their glamorous new guest.

'The ball we went to in Evansdale earlier this year. Honor was one of the organisers,' Adam said smoothly, turning back to Helen to change the subject. 'It was certainly good of you to make the effort to call on Honor. She's fortunate to have such a thoughtful and caring sister—and such an incredibly beautiful one, of course...'

'Why, thank you,' murmured Helen, shyly lowering her incredibly long lashes. Helen, who had never been shy in her life! thought Honor resentfully.

'Since she's been made so welcome by my family I think it's only fair that I get a chance to get to know hers a little better, don't you?' Adam flicked a sly glance at Honor on his right before propping his chin on his hand, the better to focus his teasing charm on the woman on the other side of him.

Honor's heart sank as Helen gave her attractive, sexy gurgle. 'Oh, better than a *little*, I hope, Adam!'

'I'm sure we'll find time in the next few days,' he murmured.

Honor's pride was singed, as well as her heart. Was he shutting her out of his attention as a sort of punishment in kind for yesterday? Or was there a more complex reason? Had he suddenly realised the mistake he would have been making if his impulsive seduction had succeeded? Or had it been seeing Helen again that brought him to his senses?

Lying in bed last night, she had been unable to stop the heated little scene between them replaying endlessly in her head. She suffered cold chills of humiliation and hot flushes of excitement every time she remembered Adam's predatory expression as he had taunted her about the letters. Excitement had dominated. His gloating triumph had not been the reaction of a man who intended to walk away and leave the fruits of victory untasted! And yet he had let *her* walk away from him, just as he had done earlier in the study. Perhaps he was confident of the sinuously tempting thoughts that he had implanted in her mind...

Honor sighed. It might all be academic, anyway, now that Helen had arrived. Just another unrealistic fantasy dreamed up by a gullible romantic. She had learned very early in her life that there was little point in trying to compete with Helen for attention—in anything. She invariably lost.

Just then, Helen glanced over Adam's half-turned shoulder at Honor, and lifted her eyebrows and widened her eyes in an instantly recognisable feminine expression that mimed a swooning 'Oh, wow' of approval.

Honor blinked, tuning abruptly back into their conversation. Then she blinked again. She couldn't believe what she was hearing!

She still couldn't believe it, half an hour later, as she helped Helen unpack dress after dress and hang them in the wardrobe of the spare bedroom next to the one she had been given for her temporary office.

'Well, sweetie, I could hardly refuse—that would have been awfully rude after his mother so generously offered to put me up...' Helen was saying, as she sat at the flounced dressing-table carrying out urgent repairs on a chipped nail while Honor trotted back and forth behind her, hanging up dresses.

'I really did do him an injustice, didn't I?' Helen giggled, her finger steady as a rock as she painted. 'I can't figure out why I didn't remember him first time round, he's such a gorgeous specimen, in a rugged sort of way. Of course, I don't normally go for rugby-forward types but he's got a nice city-slick about him, too...' She looked up from her artistry and saw Honor's expression reflected in the mirror.

'Oh, come on, Hon, you can't really object to me going out with him?' she pouted. 'It's only dinner, for goodness' sake, and he said you had some silly old deadline you had to work on. I'm only going to be here a couple of days, so where's the harm ... ?'

Honor didn't feel like mentioning the Blake males' reputation for whirlwind courtships. Nor did she intend telling her sister that there was no work Honor had to do tonight—no deadline that couldn't wait a few days. Adam had just invented that as an excuse to get Helen off alone—or had it been a sop to Honor's wounded pride?

'Anyway, you know how hopeless you are with men. This way I get to check him out for you...'

'Now that is the *feeblest* excuse for accepting a date with a man that I've *ever* heard you give,' said Honor, torn between resigned laughter and the violent desire to shake her sister until her perfect teeth rattled.

Helen laughed shamelessly. 'OK, so I think he's a hunk and can't resist the chance to find out if he's as charming as he thinks he is. But how charming can he be? Even *I* have rules about a first date, you know. Now why don't you pick out something suitably demure for me to wear, so you won't have to worry about your golden-haired boy being driven mad with requited lust at the mere sight of me?'

'That's *unrequited*, Helen,' corrected Honor, giving up the unequal battle.

'Oh, right—keep reminding me of that, won't you…?'

Secretly, Honor had been hoping that Adam might seek her out with reassurances, but she was disappointed and at lunchtime Sara told her that he had left for an afternoon meeting with representatives from the Ministry of Agriculture and Fisheries in town. At six he telephoned from Auckland and told Helen that he was running late, and asked her if she would mind meeting him directly at the restaurant, a twenty-minute taxi ride away.

Even draped neck to toe in a simple, straight grey silk sheath that had looked like a nun's habit on the clothes-hanger, Helen looked like a goddess. Honor watched her get into her taxi at seven o'clock with a panicky feeling that she had made a dreadful mistake. She shouldn't have let Helen treat this dinner like a joke. She shouldn't have let Adam get away with dismissing her like yesterday's news. Oh, what a stupid, spineless coward she was!

Five hours later the fear had solidified into mournful certainty as she paced back and forth in Helen's empty room, pausing every now and then to peek through the curtains.

Damn it, where could they *be* at this hour?

Scrub that. She didn't really want to know. What if they had booked into a hotel? What if they had gone to Kowhai Hill, knowing it was empty?

What if they had turned her home into their private love-nest for the night?

The horrifying thought took root and rapidly grew into a choking vine. When she realised she was actually seriously considering jumping into her newly resuscitated VW and driving over there at breakneck speed to catch them *in flagrante delicto* Honor decided she was driving herself mad and fled back to the sanctuary of her own room.

Grimly she selected the sexiest piece of lingerie she owned—a sheer black silk teddy with contoured lace cups that made the most of her considerable cleavage and lacing down the front that was a wicked counterpoint to the modest little frill of lace flirting over her hips. If Helen could swan around in silk, then so could her sister!

She got into the bed and turned off the light. She turned it on again and adjusted her pillow. She pushed down the quilt because she was too hot, then dragged it up again. She closed her eyes to keep the tears in.

She was just considering the drastic remedy of counting sheep when she heard the quiet purr of an expensive engine outside followed by faint bangs and crunches and then hushed sounds from within the house. Honor was sure that her acutely tuned hearing could detect every individual tuft of carpet compressing and expanding again under their creeping feet.

Adam's door quietly opened and closed.

A tiny rustle of silk sounded outside Honor's door. It had the impact of a fire alarm. She was out of bed in a flash, slammed on the light and ripped open the door.

Helen froze like a doe in a spotlight, her shoes dangling from her hand, her skirt lifted to mid-calf as she wobbled on one bare foot in the pool of light shafting from Honor's room. Her luminous green eyes had a glazed expression. One beautiful sister, slightly foxed, thought Honor, cresting a new wave of violent outrage. Her lipstick had worn off, too. Doing what? Honor wondered wretchedly.

'What time do you call *this*?' she hissed at her furiously.

'I——'

'Do you know what *time* it is?' Her whisper rose perilously towards a squeak as she dragged her thirty-year-old sister into the room like a defiant teenager.

'Well, I——'

'Do you *know* what *time* it is?' Honor repeated, vibrating like a tuning fork with rage. 'Where in the *hell* have you been until this hour? And don't tell me the restaurant—it closed over two hours ago!'

Helen leaned closer, trying to focus on Honor's furious face. 'How did you know that?'

Honor stepped back and crossed her arms over her stomach, causing her sister's mouth to drop open as she took in the full effect of the black teddy.

'Honor, where did you get that incredible outfit? You look quite—quite . . . well, *sexy* . . .'

She had no need to sound so taken aback! 'Because I telephoned the restaurant and they told me, that's how!' she said fiercely.

'You—telephoned—the restaurant?' Helen repeated slowly, shaking her head to try and improve her comprehension.

Honor didn't even blush. 'Yes, I telephoned the restaurant,' she bit off. 'And they said you weren't there!'

Helen pouted. It wasn't half so effective on unpainted lips, thought Honor critically. 'That was because we left to go somewhere else for dessert.'

'For *two hours*?'

'It was an all-night place. Chocolate a speciality, but of course I only had the fresh fruit salad. We were so busy talking, time just got away from us and——'

'Oh, really?' Honor interrupted sarcastically.

'It's the truth! Why're you so mad? Did you finish your work early or something?'

It was finally getting through to Helen that there was something drastically different about her sister, and it wasn't just what she was wearing!

'Why did you do it?' Honor demanded, planting her hands on her hips in aggressive demand, having no idea of the wildly exotic image she presented. 'You *knew* I didn't want you to go out with him but you went anyway. It was just a bit of a laugh to you. Well, it wasn't to me and I'm warning you now: lay off.'

'Honor——'

'That's the last time you go *anywhere* with Adam Blake, even if he grovels to you on bended knees. *Comprenez*?'

'Well, I——'

'This is the one man in the entire world who's not available to you. OK? Even if he *thinks* he is, I'm telling you that he's not. Not today. Not tomorrow. Not within your lifetime. Are you getting the message now? Whatever happens between him and me makes no difference: he's off limits—*forever*. Find some other hunk to amuse you. I was here first. This one is *mine*.'

'Uh—Honor——'

Honor wasn't ready to stop. 'Back off!'

'Look, Honor——'

'No, *you* look——'

'Can I look, too?'

The low, silken drawl came from the vicinity of the adjoining door behind her. Honor turned slowly and Helen said apologetically, 'I did try to tell you, sweetie, but you were stuck at full throttle. He's been there pretty well all along...'

Honor didn't hear her, or see her shrug of tipsy resignation at Adam before she slipped out the door.

'That was quite some speech...'

Adam's hands were in the trouser pockets of the dark blue suit he had worn out of the house that morning. Lounging against the door-jamb, he was making no attempt to hide his blatantly sexual study of her lush, provocatively framed figure. 'Did you mean it?'

Honor tossed her head, which unbeknown to her had an interesting flow-on effect down the rest of her body. 'What do you think?'

His eyes were pure gold and dead sober. 'I think you're a sinfully attractive woman.'

She was disappointed in him. She glared proudly. 'You don't have to lie to me——'

'You attract me, therefore you must be attractive,' he pointed out with seductive logic, taking his hands out of his pockets as he shouldered off the edge of the door and sauntered towards her. 'And in that sexy bit of nothing you're definitely an invitation to sin. Are you extending that invitation to me tonight, darling? I do hope so, because I have every intention of accepting...'

She stared at him, half hypnotised by the frank appreciation of his words and the glitter of sensuous determination in his eyes. He looked down, smoothing his hands over the warm upper swells of her breasts where they were lifted and separated by the soft boning of the basque-style bodice. Then his fingers traced down the narrow strip of skin revealed by the lacing to her indented navel, where he inserted his thumb and withdrew it, and repeated the action, stretching the tiny, shallow cavity with a series of wickedly suggestive thrusts that flooded her womb with warmth.

Much as she would have liked to melt, she couldn't, she wouldn't. 'About Helen...' she forced herself to say.

'Apart from drinking a glass or two more than she should have, your sister behaved impeccably—and so did I. She is an interesting woman, but not my type. You are. So I asked her all about you and she told me. At length. She told me all about you from the day you disrupted her tranquil, self-centred, childish existence by arriving home a squalling, chubby-cheeked cherub in *her* mother's arms to your present, quiet, sedate self. But you don't look anything like a cherub tonight and you certainly look anything but sedate...'

His voice drifted down an octave as he watched his finger trace the tiny bow that fastened the lacing between her breasts. 'Why wouldn't you look at me when you introduced Helen this morning?' He lifted one end of the bow on the pad of his finger.

She didn't realise he had been aware of her rigid defensiveness. 'Because I knew what I would see...'

'Did you? Or were just so afraid of what you *might* see, you preferred not to look at all...?'

Honor was finding it hard to breathe. If he played with that end of the bow for much longer it would...

It unravelled with a little rush.

'Oh,' he said softly, with mock-dismay. 'Look what's happened. What shall I do now?'

'What do you want to do?' asked Honor shakily, feeling that the world had shifted on its axis for the second time today.

'I want to lay you down and make sweet, slow love to you for what's left of the night...'

'Oh.' His passionate simplicity stole even more breath from her throat. She cleared it awkwardly, and said nothing, wondering belatedly whether the exotic boldness of her lingerie had badly misled him as to her experience.

He took her hand and backed away, leading her gently into his room, but instead of drawing her into his arms immediately he asked curiously, 'Why wait until tonight to deliver that lecture to Helen? Why didn't you say something this morning?'

'I—is that what I was supposed to do?' Honor asked, a little trill of pleasure skipping along her nerves as Adam slowly loosened his tie and took it off. Then he removed his jacket and his pale blue shirt, never taking his eyes off her flushed face. 'Did you want me to act like a jealous bitch?'

'Why not—you were, weren't you?'

As she shifted her head nervously, her eyes caught the light, their colour intensifying. His hands paused on his belt-buckle.

'Very green-eyed,' he confirmed in a low husk of amusement. 'You disguised it very well at the time; I thought you didn't care or you would have called my bluff and invited yourself along, so that I'd have a chance to show you that she leaves me cold. I would have loved some indication that you were prepared to fight for me. There's nothing wrong with being jealous of a lover. After all, *I'm* jealous...'

Honor's lips parted in surprise. 'Of what?'

'Of this...' He ran his hand caressingly up the front of the teddy to where her breasts crowded the silk. 'Of everything you wear next to your skin. That's where I want to be. And I'm jealous of Helen and all the other people who know more about you than I do—especially the men...' He boldly stripped his belt from his waist and lowered his zip before pulling her close and shuddering. 'Touch me, Honor. Put your hands on my chest...'

There was one more thing she had to settle first, even though it was becoming as hard to think as it was to breathe.

'Adam—about Helen...'

'I told you——'

'No, not *mine*, the other one. The Helen you fell in love with and wrote those letters to...'

'You mean Mary?'

'Not your wife—*Helen*.' She wondered whether the same desire that smoked along her senses and obscured her thoughts had also clouded his.

'But Mary *was* Helen...Helen was *Mary*. My God, didn't I ever tell you that?' he murmured, in as much shock as she. 'It was a sort of a joke between us—she was my Helen of Troy, I was her Paris—kidnapping her love from her parents and carrying her off for myself.

Which is exactly what I did. Her parents disapproved of our marriage—she was an only child and they thought Mary was too young and I was too big and rough, too hot-blooded and disrespectful ever to be suitable for their delicate little girl. They disapproved of me until the day they died. I could never forgive myself for being the reason that Mary was alienated from her parents, even though she never once threw it up at me...'

Honor's unfurling confidence froze, darkening her sea-green eyes with doubts. Could she still go through with this? According to Greek legend Helen was the most beautiful woman of her entire age! Everything she learnt about Mary-Helen seemed designed to make Honor feel lack-lustre and ordinary.

And yet Adam didn't think of her that way...

'I wrote those letters in a rage of hormones—I stole bits from great literature because I didn't think I could match their fluent skill in seduction,' he murmured, picking up her wrists in his strong hands, as if he sensed her uncertainty and was focusing sharply in on it.

'But *you* didn't have to cheat like that, Honor, because you have an incredibly sensuous response to words and a romantic nature that makes you instinctively know how to use them. When I read some of the things you said it was like being stroked with a velvet glove. I got aroused, and I knew that you had been aroused when you wrote them for me, too...'

In that same, sultry voice he quoted her one of her wilder paragraphs. 'I like the idea that I can inspire you to write something like that...'

Honor's captive pulse beat heavily against his palms. 'It wasn't so much you as your letters,' she denied huskily.

'You were absorbed by the rapture of your love,' he said, lifting her hands to the level of his chest. 'And that love was embodied in every lustrous word...' He dipped to kiss first one wrist, and then the other in tender salute.

'*Lust*rous being exactly the right word.' Honor tried to keep the last fragment of her pride intact with the foolish pun. 'It was a physical infatuation expressed in metaphysical form——'

'You fell in love with a phantom.' He mocked her refusal to admit it. 'And now you need him to love you back.'

She wouldn't let him see how devoutly she wished it. He might want to tease her into saying it, but she wouldn't be able to say it as teasingly as he wanted her to. She couldn't. And her serious intensity might very well drive him away...

'I want him to *make* love to me.' She made the distinction boldly. 'But he seems more interested in wordplay than love-play. Do you usually make it so difficult for a woman to start an affair with you?'

His face was unreadably still. 'An affair...is that really all you expect from me, Honor?' Was that a trace of anxiety in his question? She rushed to reassure him.

'Of course it is. Friends *and* lovers, you said.' She pushed against his restraining fingers, until her hands could flatten against his hard chest. 'Or have you changed *your* mind?'

His nostrils flared as he watched her breasts lift with the act of placing her palms on the thick pelt of his chest hair, the blue veins on their surface becoming more prominent as blood flowed under her skin, engorging them with a heavy ripeness.

'So be it.' His hands covered hers for a moment, pressing them against his hot chest, then moved to bracket her hips, pulling her hard into the cradle of his hips with a groan of relief.

'Oh, yes, *yes* . . .' His head tilted back as she raked her nails lightly against him. 'Harder, Honor, I need to really *feel* you! To know you're real. Like this . . . touch me like this . . .'

His fingers had found her nipples through the stiff cups of lace, drawing them out with gentle twists that sent ribbons of fire unfurling through her body. When she copied him, seeking out the flat masculine areolae in their nests of soft curling hair, he shuddered violently and Honor was stunned to feel them harden and thrust eagerly against her caressing fingers.

'Oh, yes, God, yes, I like that...do that again, harder—and this, do this to me, too...' He bent his head and her body leapt in shocked pleasure as she felt him run his open mouth over the twin curves of her breasts straining above the black lace. He pressed his face deep into the abundant softness and rubbed it back and forth. The sensation of him crushing and kneading her and then biting and sucking moistly at the creamy mounds was profoundly and primitively erotic.

He cupped her head when she feverishly sought reciprocal rights, shifting her mouth against his chest, guiding her for his pleasure while his hands explored beneath the frill that veiled the shadowed mound between her legs and the high rise of her buttocks. For long, sumptuous moments they shuddered and fought against the restrictions of being a single desire in two separate human bodies, until Adam uttered a harsh sound of impatience and twisted away to rake the rest of his clothing down his hard thighs.

He stood before her, naked and unashamed, magnificently aroused, his muscles thick and corded, bulging with a brutal tension that screamed for release. Honor's eyes were momentarily stunned with admiration until she saw how his swollen body reacted to her silent worship, shifting and hardening even further in a way that terrified and excited her. She trembled as she guided his big hand back to the trailing laces that hung down the front of the teddy.

He was swift to interpret her shy request. 'This lacing must be uncomfortably tight...' he suggested softly, pulling it momentarily tighter, the compression delivering a sexual jolt to her highly sensitised nerve-endings.

Honor watched him under heavy lids, responding as she knew he wanted her to. 'Yes, yes, it is...very...'

'Would you like me to ease it for you?'

'That would be nice,' she said breathlessly.

He sat her on the edge of the bed and knelt at her feet, applying delicate pressure on her knees to part them and, moving boldly into the space he had created, began unlacing her with a deliberately tormenting slowness, holding the two edges of the teddy together as he removed the ties from their lace eyelets.

'Now... let's see if I can relieve that painful discomfort,' he murmured thickly, slowly peeling the bodice away, tugging it roughly apart at the last to burst the snaps that fastened the narrow band of silk between her legs. The sharp, satiny friction made her gasp and to her shock he touched her lightly there, a teasing stroke of a finger against her parted softness. She moaned.

'Did I hurt you?'

She shook her head mutely, her mouth too dry to talk.

'There, does that feel better now that there's nothing here to bind you?' He traced the faint impression of a seam down her side. She seemed to quiver all over, her softly rounded nudity acutely receptive to the sight and scent of his aroused masculinity. She was utterly his, and he knew it.

She licked her lips. 'A... little.'

A carnal expression of satisfaction burned in his eyes at the sound of her husky challenge. 'Only a little? Then let me see if I can do a lot better...'

He groaned, but not with effort, as he lifted her with easy strength to lay her flat on the bed, her bent knee brushing his rigidly swaying length as he moved over her, settling between her restless legs.

Her hands reached for his lean male hips but he drew them away. 'No, not yet, darling, I want you readier for me than this...and if you touch me now I'll explode. Here...hold on, darling—promise you'll hold on tight for me...'

He wrapped his big hands around hers and lifted them to the vertical bars of the bedstead, curling her fingers around the thin cylinders of cold brass and holding them there so that her arms were outstretched over her head, her torso lightly arched over the thick, soft pillow under her shoulders as he bent to his self-appointed task.

'No, don't let go,' he growled, long, agonising minutes later as he slid further down her perspiration-slicked body, and Honor's hands clenched violently on the brass as she felt his first, delicate, exploring touch.

'That's right, arch your body, move with me, but whatever you do, darling, don't let go!'

'Adam——!' The cry was wrenched from the depths of her bewilderment.

'No, let me do this...let me be selfish...I want to see it happen to you first before I take you. I want you to be as sweet and ripe inside as you are here, and here...and here...'

Honor needed her cold brass anchor to reality as her whole world splintered and formed and reformed around her, around the slow, languid, flicker and lash of his tongue and the hot, hazy pooling of pleasure created in the dips and hollows of her body by his big, capable hands. The slow, thick pulsation of her heart moved from her chest to the place between her parted thighs, where all sensation began and ended...with Adam.

Suddenly Honor cried out, her whole body contracting, her hips lifting from the bed in a violent series of wrenching convulsions as she was cast into a turbulent new realm of experience. At the instant the first paroxysm hit Adam cried out her name in a savage shout of triumphant exhilaration and reared up, coming down with a powerfully driving thrust that obliterated her last conscious thought, stretching and filling her, lifting and plunging again and again as he rode her to an ecstatic completion. His own culmination was just as turbulent and violently fulfilling and seemed to go on forever.

And afterwards, a long time afterwards, when light was streaming in through the chinks in the curtains, and he had made love to her twice more—each time urging her to more reckless heights of passion—he grimly asked the question that had hovered silently in the air above their heads since the first moment of his possession.

'Why the hell didn't you warn me I was going to be your first lover?'

CHAPTER TEN

IT WAS strange how much more a tone could convey the words themselves, thought Honor, hideously graunching the VW's new gears as she changed down in order to lurch up another winding hill.

If Adam had held her in his arms and asked his all-important question with tender curiosity she wouldn't be driving home now, making the reckless flight that she had contemplated last night—for very different reasons.

But he hadn't. He had rolled away from her on to his back, spoken with a brusqueness that verged on anger, edged with something that sounded chillingly like regret. And, too, he had used 'warn' rather than 'tell'. To warn someone was usually to notify them of possible danger ahead. What possible danger could her innocence have been to Adam? How could something that had seemed so beautifully right turn out to be so ugly and wrong?

'Why the hell didn't you warn me I was going to be your first lover?'

Honor had reached down to pull a corner of the rumpled quilt across her body, suddenly embarrassed by her wanton sprawl.

'I said I *had* chances, not that I ever took them,' she replied quietly.

'A virgin. At *your* age!' he muttered in brooding disbelief tinged with...was it contempt? No, that was too strong, it was more like angry disappointment.

Oh, God—he was disappointed!

Honor cringed. He had expected something extraordinary from her and she had given him only her very ordinary self. She had probably been clumsy and inept

171

compared to his flawless Mary-Helen. He had made love to her three times, each time more fiercely than the last, but maybe that hadn't been because her eager response had inspired him to ever greater passion, as she had naïvely imagined, but because he had been desperate to find the fulfilment that had been promised by the sizzling sexual tension that had built up between them. Only there was no true fulfilment, only a bitter emptiness that prompted an angry questioning of what had gone wrong.

She had to face it. What she had felt he had not shared. What had been sublimely unique to her had been commonplace to him.

Glory folded its splendid wings and quietly slipped away.

'Maybe I am a bit of an anachronism these days,' she said stiffly, 'but I vowed when I was a teenager that I'd never end up like Helen's jet-set model friends. If that was the way sophisticated people behaved I didn't want any part of it. To them sex was as casual and meaningless as a handshake.' Her voice shook as she said it. 'To me it was going to be something special...'

'And this is it?' She flinched at his savagery as he rolled over and cynically surveyed the way she was hugging the bedclothes tightly against her body. 'This is your "something special"? A pity you didn't feel the need to make it "special" for me, too... why? Didn't you trust me? What the hell did you think I'd *do*——?'

'I didn't think it mattered...' she lied weakly.

'Didn't matter?' He exploded upright on the bed, totally oblivious to his state of undress as he turned towards her and demanded, 'What the hell did you bother keeping your virginity for, if you were going to throw it away like this? Talk about casual! My God, Honor, not even you could be that stupid—of course it *matters*! You weren't even prepared, were you, you little fool? If I hadn't had the presence of mind to ask if you were protected you would have risked getting pregnant your very first time! Or is that what you wanted to make it even more *special* for yourself...?'

She clenched her hands over her chest, flushing at his cutting anger. Now at least some of that fury was explained. He was right, she *had* been foolish; her obsession with loving him had blinded her to the true consequences of her actions. She couldn't believe her usual level-headed self could have been so careless as to forget the prime biological reason for the human sex drive...procreation. No wonder he thought she might have had notions of trapping him...

'I—it's the wrong time of the month for me...' she told him truthfully, at the same time wondering whether her forgetfulness *had* been a subconscious attempt to bind herself to him in some permanent way...

His hardening expression told her what he thought of that time-honoured prevarication. 'It's the wrong time for you, full stop!' he told her tautly. 'Do you think if I'd *known* I'd have allowed it to happen this way?'

The confirmation of her worst fears was a blow that couldn't be avoided. She took it on the chin and struck back.

'What way? I didn't know there was any other way for a man and woman to make love——'

Her sarcasm rebounded painfully on herself. 'No, you didn't, did you? And that's the point. There are a lot of things you don't know or didn't bother to find out.' His eyes made a grim survey of her shielded body. 'Did I hurt you? Are you sore?'

To her horror he put his hand on the quilt as if he intended to whisk away her defences and check her as clinically as any doctor.

'*No!*'

'I must have; you were very tight that first time——'

Her flush deepened, anger conquering her humiliation. 'That didn't stop you, though, did it? Why didn't you ask me *then* if it mattered to you so much? Why wait until you've had all your fun to worry about whether you hurt me or not?'

It was his turn to flush, his eyes darkening to mid-brown as he gritted, 'It wasn't *fun*——'

'Oh, no, I could see you hated every minute of it,' she said fiercely. How dared he imply that he hadn't enjoyed what they'd done at all? It might not have been earth-shattering as far as he was concerned but it hadn't been the nothing he was trying to dismiss it as, either!

'You're deliberately misunderstanding me...'

'Oh, I'm so sorry, but then we stupidly naïve virgins tend to do that——'

'You'd better learn to start speaking in the past tense there, Honor. You gave your virginity to me, remember?'

She flared quickly at his insulting tone. 'Yes, and what a mistake *that* was. I should have kept it for someone who would appreciate the—the——' She hesitated, trying to think of the appropriate word.

He provided it for her in a cruel pun. 'The *honour*?'

She took a deep breath. 'As it happens I regret it, too... all in all the whole thing was a bit of an anti-climax, wasn't it?' She almost choked on her small, bitter laugh. She looked longingly over her shoulder towards the door but she couldn't force herself to move. She couldn't imitate his unselfconscious nudity. The idea of getting out of bed under his critical stare was unendurable.

Adam made a soft sound. 'Damn it, Honor, that's not what I meant to say... why do you goad me into these things by pretending to be blasé when we both know you're not?

'You took me by surprise... is it so difficult to appreciate how much? I couldn't believe it that first time, and when I did you were right—I was too selfishly absorbed in my own pleasure to care. I wanted to grab what I could while I could, to have something to hold

on to when the recriminations started. I *never* said I
was disappointed. Did I *feel* disappointed when I was
inside you? Damn it, *look* at me!' His hand cupped her
averted jaw and forced her face back to his, his palm
cool against her flushed cheek. His eyes were deep and
dark and compelling, filled with repressed emotion.
Unfortunately his earnest assurances were coming just
that little bit too late to be convincing.

'You must see that I had every reason to think that
you knew exactly what you were getting into...'

'Of course I knew,' she said flippantly, her green eyes
meeting his proudly. 'I was getting into bed with you.'

'You were doing a hell of a lot more than that, Honor,'
he informed her harshly. 'This was never going to be a
one-night stand for either of us. You said you wanted
an affair—and then I find that you can't possibly know
the first thing about the risks an affair entails. And even
knowing that I still took advantage of your inexperi-
ence——'

Guilt. She might have known it! Well, she didn't want
his guilt or his sympathy. Neither was a substitute for
love. And neither was desire, she now realised. Desire
without love had no strength, no substance to cling to
when times got rough...

'You don't have to wor——'

She broke off as there was a soft knock at his door,
rolling over on her side to stare at it in horror.

Adam recovered first. Pulling part of the quilt over
his hips, he called out, 'Who is it?' He anchored Honor's
precious covering with his arm over her waist as she instinctively made to leave, dragging her back against his
curved torso so that she felt the soft crush of thick chest
hair cushioning her sensitive skin. 'No, don't you dare
move until this is settled!' he growled, not bothering to
lower his voice.

There was a little pause, then a subdued voice drifted
through the wood panels. 'It's Tania. I'm going into town

to look at apartments this morning and wanted to know if——'

Honor was shocked when Adam called out again, 'For goodness' sake, you don't have to yell it through the door, Tania. Come on in.'

'*Adam*——!' Honor's horrified retreat beneath the shared quilt wasn't quick enough. The door opened before she had covered more than her chin.

To her credit Tania didn't say a word, even though her shock was palpable. Neither did she take up Adam's invitation and step inside. She just looked, her eyebrows raised in a way that implied that whoever she had expected to find in Adam's bed it hadn't been Honor. Helen, most probably. After all, with a swan around why would Adam want to bother with an ugly duckling?

Tania shrugged in cool resignation. 'I just wanted some advice, that's all. But I can see you're very busy.'

Honor felt her whole body tingle as Adam's lips suddenly brushed the top of her bare shoulder in a tacit acknowledgement of the sarcastic comment. 'You obviously see very clearly. Call my construction office and get Don Shelly's number—he's my property lawyer, he handles all kinds of real estate and can give you far better advice than I can... I'm afraid at the moment I find my concentration severely impaired.'

Tania looked along the hall and then back at Adam, smiling brilliantly. 'Thank you, Adam. I wonder if you'll still look quite as disgustingly smug in a few moments from now?' And with that she turned on her heel and walked away.

Adam's arm tightened across the quilt as Honor tensed, wondering what on earth Tania had meant. She didn't have to wait long.

Perversely, in her school uniform, Sara actually looked older than her twelve years. Her expression was equally mature as she looked at Honor's bare shoulders protectively framed by her father's bare chest, the quilt cuddled around their closely pressed bodies.

'Hi.' She came across the room to bounce on the edge of the bed, eyeing them with mischievous curiosity. 'What are you doing?'

'OK, brat, there's no need to try and embarrass me into asking Honor to marry me,' her father told her sternly, but Honor felt the laughter rumbling against her spine. How could he laugh at a time like this? she thought, too shocked to take in fully what he was saying. 'As it happens I'm just about to do it. We've been having a private discussion leading up to the subject, with the emphasis on *private*, and we haven't finished it yet. So buzz off while we finish it, will you?'

'Discussion, huh?' Sara whooped, bouncing off the bed again and winking at Honor's pale face. 'I knew it would happen. I just knew it would! You love each other, right?'

'Too right.' Adam's arm contracted painfully at Honor's convulsive movement, but nothing could have hurt more than the excruciating pain in her chest. This must be what a heart attack feels like, she thought through the mist of agony.

'And you're gonna get married and everything?' she dimly heard Sara say happily.

'Especially the everything,' said Adam wickedly, nipping at the side of Honor's throat, not seeming to notice her deathly stillness. Moments later when Sara had skipped out of the door she had torn herself out of his arms and thrown off the quilt, her modesty forgotten in her anguish...

Honor saw her white picket fence through blurring eyes. The relief was enormous. She had been right to come home, she thought, as she parked the VW crookedly in the short driveway and stumbled out.

Adam hadn't understood her numb refusal to listen to his glib explanations. He hadn't understood what he had done by pretending to love her for the sake of his daughter, not until she had finally turned on him and flung his humiliating lie about wanting to marry her in his face.

'We both know what you want and it isn't a wife you're madly in love with!' she'd accused wildly when he had doggedly followed her into her room and refused to leave while she dressed. Cornered like an animal, she'd lashed out.

'Oh, yes, it's fine for you if she's in love with *you*... that makes it all so much easier for you. And isn't it terrific if she's a Plain Jane who'll be so grateful for any attention at all that she won't mind playing second fiddle to a blasted *ghost*? You're not capable of loving anyone who's *alive*. If I were beautiful or vivacious I might be competition for your goddess-like Helen of Troy and you wouldn't like that—that would be like being unfaithful to her. It wouldn't matter that you were being unfaithful to *me*. What do I matter? I'm just someone who happened along to fit the bill as Sara's mother and your bed-warmer. A *friend* who could be relied on not to get too emotionally demanding...'

She laughed bitterly at his expression of shock, pleased that she had finally penetrated through his thick skin. 'No wonder you were so appalled to find out I was a virgin; I wouldn't have had much to recommend me if I hadn't been good in bed, would I? How lucky I managed to pass the test after all!'

'Is it so difficult to believe that I've fallen in love with you?' Adam asked quietly, but her rage was a thunder in her ears, drowning out the emotion behind the calm words.

Honor's laughter was wild with despair. 'The way you fell in love with your first wife, your one and *only* wife? Oh, is that why you sent me all those love-letters and plied me with sweet nothings and were so proud to be my first lover? Oh, yes, Adam, you were so-o-o convincing...!'

Honor's hand shook as she fitted her key to the front door, almost falling over the threshold in her haste to get inside.

She had brought nothing with her, she realised with a weird sense of detachment as she walked through the silent rooms. She had started to pack but then Helen had come in and began talking to her in that slow, aggravatingly calm voice as if she were trying to communicate with a half-wit. Honor knew that Adam had sent her—everyone was on his side, no one on hers— and had succeeded in completely ignoring her until Helen had started taking things out of her suitcase as fast as she put them in.

'This is absolutely ridiculous! I hope you don't expect me to come with you—I didn't come all this way to spend it packing and unpacking. I have to leave tomorrow, you know—I'll be sued for breach of contract if I don't. I can't hang around here and watch you ruin your life for the sake of a stupid little misunderstanding that could be cleared up in an instant. It's as plain as the nose on your face that you're in love with the man.' Honor winced at the unhappy metaphor. 'And if he claims he loves you, why look a gift horse in the mouth? Why don't you give the poor guy a break...?'

And so it had gone on and on until Honor had abandoned her methodical attempt at departure and simply fled. She needed desperately to get home, back to her sanctuary, where she would be safe, protected by the comfort of familiar possessions and surroundings, wallowing in the misery of solitude...

So now she was here she had no luggage, no computer, no wallet and there wasn't any food in the house. She had even abandoned Monty—not that he was likely to notice that she was gone from his over-pampered existence at the Blakes'. She would probably never be able to entice him home again . . . Another loss she could lay at Adam's door.

She wandered through to the lounge and sat at her empty desk, looking out through the French doors at the spring colour that was blooming in her garden.

She could see bees floating lazily on the air above the nodding flowers, like giant motes of dust. She didn't know how long she sat there in a semi-trance—it could have been hours—but the state of tranquil acceptance that Honor sought never came. Adam's face kept intruding, and Sara's—bright with loving glee that her desperate measures hadn't been in vain after all, and Joy's as she had last seen it, frowning anxiously as Honor had rushed past her out of the door, throwing herself into her car and driving away with a defiant spurt of gravel.

The desk drawer that had held her letters was still slightly ajar and she pulled it out, inevitably remembering that first night and the outrage she had felt to come back and find Adam rifling through her belongings. She touched the bottom of the empty drawer wistfully. Adam was always outraging her, in writing and in person, challenging her to think, to argue, to find some way to challenge him back. Even in bed he had challenged her to excite him.

But this time she had no heart for the fight. She had lost it last night, along with her courage and her sense of humour, not to mention her wretched virginity. If only she had been a complete slut—she probably would have eloped with Adam by now instead of being held hostage by her ridiculous scruples about love! She smiled faintly; perhaps she hadn't quite lost her sense of humour after all . . .

When her doorbell rang she found she hadn't lost her heart either, because it began thumping madly. But when she looked out of the window she discovered that it wasn't a smoking Mercedes parked behind her in the

driveway but a light blue van she didn't recognise. Damn
it, did she really expect Adam to come running round
after her entreating her to change her mind? He was
probably glad she had let him off the hook!

Her steps dragged as she answered the door to find a
lanky, gum-chewing young stranger waiting impatiently.
He raised his clipboard and pen.

'You Miss Honor Sheldon?'

'Yes.'

'Honor *Leigh* Sheldon?'

'Yes.'

'The Honor Leigh Sheldon who works for the
Evansdale Advertiser?'

'*Yes!*' Now it was Honor who was impatient. 'Yes,
that's me. What are you doing, conducting a survey?'
With her current run of luck it would be a survey of
local virgins.

'Sign here.'

'Why?' she asked dully.

'Because I have a package for you, that's why, and
you have to sign for it.'

'What package?' Belatedly she noticed the name of a
courier company, painted on the side of the van.

The envelope he made her sign for was a plain, A4
manila with no address or identification on the outside,
save the courier's serial number.

'What is it?' she wondered out loud, turning it over
in her hands.

'Don't ask me, I only deliver 'em,' the young man
shrugged. 'But in case it's a letter-bomb I think I'll leave
you to it.'

He was chuckling at his mortuary humour as he
walked away, and Honor gave her door a little slam as
she went back inside, to show him what his customers
thought of his feeble jokes.

The envelope was sealed so she went back to her desk
and used her silver letter-opener to slit the seal. It slipped,

nearly cutting her finger, and the contents of the envelope spilled out over the blotter. They were photographs and Honor sifted through the first two disinterestedly.

People often sent her colour photographs, hoping they would make the newspaper's social events page, but these were even less usable than most. The woman, the same one in both pictures, was wearing clothing almost the same colour as the indistinct background, into which she would probably recede completely if converted to black and white for the paper. She had short, wavy, mouse-brown hair and a cowlick on one side that wouldn't sit down. Spectacles sat on her button nose, and her wide, friendly smile was spoiled by slightly crooked front teeth.

Honor fanned through the other pictures and was surprised to see they were mostly of the same woman involved in various outdoor activities that showed off a pear-shaped figure that might have been considered the feminine ideal—three hundred years ago. Honor sympathised with the picture of the woman in a swimsuit, although she didn't appear to be self-conscious, laughing with the small child frolicking in the water beside her, a chubby child with straggly blonde hair and big eyes that...

Honor looked harder. She looked from the child to the woman. She scrabbled among the photographs until she burnt her fingers on one in which the woman, pregnant this time, had a male escort, a big, husky man who towered over her as he held her in the crook of his long arm...

The tingling flame shot up Honor's arms and coagulated in her chest, burning even more fiercely as she slowly turned the photograph over. There, written in age-faded blue ink in a hand she knew as well as her own, was scrawl:

Mary and I at the Hannigans' Harvest Dance. Mary's varicose veins wouldn't let her cut up wild on the floor as usual!

Honor raised her hands to her mouth and pressed them there, closing her eyes briefly.

Mary. Helen of Troy. Two women as dissimilar as it was possible for them to be.

No wonder Adam had said it was a joke between them. Mary was painfully plain. But loved—very much loved...and very loving. It shone out of her eyes and her face; even in the unsmiling shots she looked happy, the supreme contentment of a woman who knew she was cherished above all others. It showed in the photographs and it showed in the brief commentaries written on the back, some addressed by name to Joy, others just a hasty notation to freeze a marvellous moment in time.

When Honor picked up the last photograph, a wedding shot of Adam with shoulder-length blonde hair slicked back and a carnation pinned to the lapel of his sports jacket and Mary wearing a white shift and clutching a small yellow posy, she was blinking away tears for the umpteenth time that day, and nearly missed the small buff envelope that had slipped under the edge of the blotter.

'Honor Leigh Sheldon'.

He was taking no chances.

It was unsealed.

'Honor, My Only Love'...

It was a love-letter. Intended for her, delivered to her. Hers alone...

'How do I love thee? Let me count the ways...'

There were twenty-seven.

Twenty-seven reasons why he loved her, and they were all his own! Not Elizabeth Barrett Browning's, nor Donne's nor Dryden's nor Shakespeare's, but Adam

Blake's...stark and exquisitely unadorned, simple yet passionately sincere.

> I have never felt as alone as I did when Mary died, as wounded and sick with grief and pain...until today. I knew I loved you but until today I don't think I really knew how much...
>
> I need you, Honor, much more than you can imagine—not for Sara, not for your glorious generosity in bed, not for your laughter, your wisdom and your wit—although all those things are certainly part of my love—but out of pure selfishness, for me...
>
> I can't let you go, not even for a day, without telling you that. I never loved you with my eyes, but with my heart and mind. If you believe nothing else, believe that. I want to love you, live with you, marry you, have children with you. I want to be that sensuous phantom lover of your creation but also the flesh-and-blood man who can turn your dreams into reality... Last night I promised you sweet and slow but I was too greedy to set the physical seal on our relationship. I lost control and I didn't keep that promise...that's why I was angry that it was your first time. I was afraid you were disappointed with me, as you were entitled to be. In truth the knowledge I was your first lover is something that I will treasure for the rest of my life...

She read it avidly, over and over again, her tears flowing as hot and as healing as the beautiful words.

This time there was no doorbell to warn her, only a faint rattle at the French doors.

Honor looked up and was instantly transported back in time. Adam, dressed in black jeans and sweater, stood outside looking in through the square panes, but instead of darkness shrouding him in mystery cruel sunshine etched the drawn lines of his face, revealing the aching uncertainty that he had set out so clearly and honestly in the letter that trembled in her hand.

The other major difference from the last time Adam had stood out there was resting stiffly in his arms, glaring balefully at Honor.

Her hands were trembling so much that it took three tries to unlock the French doors, by which time Monty's tail was beginning to twitch angrily against the rough black denim of Adam's jeans.

Adam looked at the letter crushed in her hand, and a faint rash of red appeared on his cheekbones. He cleared his throat. 'I thought if you could love an arrogant, bad-tempered, selfish, ill-mannered character like Monty enough to share your life with him you might find it in your heart also to share it with me. Although I don't think I'm *quite* as bad as he is; at least I won't bring dead rats into the house...'

'Oh, Adam...' Honor smiled through her tears, recognising his humour for the defence mechanism it was.

'You're crying, I'm—— Ouch, you horrible beast! Damn it, I had this touching love scene all rehearsed— ouch—hold this monster for a moment, will you, while I get his claws out of my sweater...?'

They disentangled the cat but in the process somehow managed deliciously to entangle themselves. As Monty leapt to the floor Adam held her close and buried his face in her hair.

'Oh, God, you're not going to make me wait for your answer, are you? You read my letter—— Was it...? Did you like it? I was so afraid I rushed it, but I needed to say everything I'd foolishly left unsaid——'

She lifted her head and stroked the roughness of his chin before stopping his nervous mouth with her fingers. He hadn't even stopped to shave before he had sat down with pen and paper and poured his life into her hands, she thought wonderingly. Then he had driven over to brave her rejection. 'It was the most beautiful thing I've ever read. I love you, Adam. I always have. It was my own insecurities that made me doubt I could mean as much to you. I was afraid to ask for what I really wanted.'

'*Always*?' His voice deepened huskily. 'Even last night?'

She looked at him with warm eyes that deepened his flush. '*Especially* last night. You were a wonderful lover, Adam.'

'Even this morning, when I was so inept——?'

'Adam, you're not going to spend the rest of our lives asking me to account for every single *moment* of my love, are you?' she chided him on a lilt of joyous laughter.

'Yes,' he said bluntly, and kissed her until she stopped laughing. 'I love to hear you say it. I'll never tire of it. I'll write you a love-letter every day of my life if that's what it takes to make you feel secure. And we won't only tell each other, we'll show each other daily, too, starting right now!'

They sank to the floor, the love-letter crushed beneath them as they communicated in a language more rich and varied than words.

Under the couch a bare metre away a fat, furry figure stopped licking its paws and started eyeing with malicious interest the shifting movements on the sunlit carpet. Slowly the massive head lowered and the solid hindquarters began to bunch and lift and the claws to flex in evil feline anticipation...

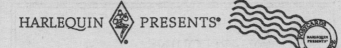

HARLEQUIN ◈ PRESENTS®

Harlequin Presents hopes you have enjoyed your year in
Europe. If you missed any of the exciting countries on the
tour, here is your opportunity to complete your collection:

Greece	#1619	*The Alpha Man* by Kay Thorpe	$2.99	☐
Italy	#1628	*Mask of Deception* by Sara Wood	$2.99	☐
Germany	#1636	*Designed To Annoy* by Elizabeth Oldfield	$2.99	☐
Spain	#1644	*Dark Sunlight* by Patricia Wilson	$2.99	☐
Belgium	#1650	*The Bruges Engagement* by Madeleine Ker	$2.99	☐
Italy	#1660	*Roman Spring* by Sandra Marton	$2.99 U.S. ☐ $3.50 CAN. ☐	
England	#1668	*Yesterday's Affair* by Sally Wentworth	$2.99 U.S. ☐ $3.50 CAN. ☐	
Portugal	#1676	*Sudden Fire* by Elizabeth Oldfield	$2.99 U.S. ☐ $3.50 CAN. ☐	
Cyprus	#1684	*The Touch of Aphrodite* by Joanna Mansell	$2.99 U.S. ☐ $3.50 CAN. ☐	
Denmark	#1691	*Viking Magic* by Angela Wells	$2.99 U.S. ☐ $3.50 CAN. ☐	
Switzerland	#1700	*No Promise of Love* by Lilian Peake	$2.99 U.S. ☐ $3.50 CAN. ☐	
France	#1708	*Tower of Shadows* by Sara Craven	$2.99 U.S. ☐ $3.50 CAN. ☐	

HARLEQUIN PRESENTS
NOT THE SAME OLD STORY!

TOTAL AMOUNT	$
POSTAGE & HANDLING	$
($1.00 for one book, 50¢ for each additional)	
APPLICABLE TAXES*	$ _____
TOTAL PAYABLE	$ _____
(check or money order—please do not send cash)	

To order, complete this form and send it, along with a check or money order for the
total above, payable to Harlequin Books, to: **In the U.S.:** 3010 Walden Avenue,
P.O. Box 9047, Buffalo, NY 14269-9047; **In Canada:** P.O. Box 613, Fort Erie, Ontario,
L2A 5X3.

Name: _____

Address: _____ City: _____

State/Prov.: _____ Zip/Postal Code: _____

*New York residents remit applicable sales taxes.
 Canadian residents remit applicable GST and provincial taxes.

HPPFE-F

HARLEQUIN®

PRESENTS Plus

When Prince Uzziah invited Beth back to his sumptuous
palace, she thought he was about to sell her the Arab
stallion of her dreams. But Uzziah had another deal on
his mind—a race...where the winner took all....

Kelda had always clashed with her stepbrother, Angelo,
but now he was interfering in her life. He claimed it was
for family reasons, and he demanded Kelda enter into a
new relationship with him—as his mistress!

What would you do if *you* were Beth or Kelda? Share
their pleasure and their passion—watch for:

Beth and the Barbarian by Miranda Lee
Harlequin Presents Plus #1711

and

Angel of Darkness by Lynne Graham
Harlequin Presents Plus #1712

Harlequin Presents Plus
The best has just gotten better!

Available in January wherever Harlequin books are sold.

PPLUS20

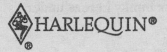 

The proprietors of Weddings, Inc. hope you
have enjoyed visiting Eternity, Massachusetts.
And if you missed any of the exciting Weddings,
Inc. titles, here is your opportunity to complete
your collection:

Harlequin Superromance	#598	*Wedding Invitation* by Marisa Carroll	$3.50 U.S. ☐ $3.99 CAN. ☐
Harlequin Romance	#3319	*Expectations* by Shannon Waverly	$2.99 U.S. ☐ $3.50 CAN. ☐
Harlequin Temptation	#502	*Wedding Song* by Vicki Lewis Thompson	$2.99 U.S. ☐ $3.50 CAN. ☐
Harlequin American Romance	#549	*The Wedding Gamble* by Muriel Jensen	$3.50 U.S. ☐ $3.99 CAN. ☐
Harlequin Presents	#1692	*The Vengeful Groom* by Sara Wood	$2.99 U.S. ☐ $3.50 CAN. ☐
Harlequin Intrigue	#298	*Edge of Eternity* by Jasmine Cresswell	$2.99 U.S. ☐ $3.50 CAN. ☐
Harlequin Historical	#248	*Vows* by Margaret Moore	$3.99 U.S. ☐ $4.50 CAN. ☐

HARLEQUIN BOOKS...
NOT THE SAME OLD STORY

TOTAL AMOUNT	$
POSTAGE & HANDLING	$
($1.00 for one book, 50¢ for each additional)	
APPLICABLE TAXES*	$
TOTAL PAYABLE	$
(check or money order—please do not send cash)	

To order, complete this form and send it, along with a check or money order for the
total above, payable to Harlequin Books, to: **In the U.S.:** 3010 Walden Avenue,
P.O. Box 9047, Buffalo, NY 14269-9047; **In Canada:** P.O. Box 613, Fort Erie, Ontario,
L2A 5X3.

Name: _____

Address: _____ City: _____

State/Prov.: _____ Zip/Postal Code: _____

*New York residents remit applicable sales taxes.
 Canadian residents remit applicable GST and provincial taxes.

WED-F

This holiday, join four hunky heroes under
the mistletoe for

Christmas Kisses

Cuddle under a fluffy quilt, with a cup of hot chocolate and these
romances sure to warm you up:

#561 HE'S A REBEL (also a Studs title)
Linda Randall Wisdom

#562 THE BABY AND THE BODYGUARD
Jule McBride

#563 THE GIFT-WRAPPED GROOM
M.J. Rodgers

#564 A TIMELESS CHRISTMAS
Pat Chandler

Celebrate the season with all four holiday books sealed with a
Christmas kiss—coming to you in December, only from
Harlequin American Romance!

CK-G

CHRISTMAS STALKINGS

All wrapped up in spine-tingling packages, here are three books guaranteed to chill your spine...and warm your hearts this holiday season!

#302 THE KID WHO STOLE CHRISTMAS
Linda Stevens

#303 I'LL BE HOME FOR CHRISTMAS
Dawn Stewardson

#304 BEARING GIFTS
Aimée Thurlo

This December, fill your stockings with the "Christmas Stalkings"—for the best in romantic suspense. Only from

HARLEQUIN®

I N T R I G U E®

HIXM

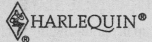

HARLEQUIN®

Don't miss these Harlequin favorites by some of our most distinguished authors!
And now you can receive a discount by ordering two or more titles!

HT#25483	BABYCAKES by Glenda Sanders	$2.99	☐
HT#25559	JUST ANOTHER PRETTY FACE by Candace Schuler	$2.99	☐
HP#11608	SUMMER STORMS by Emma Goldrick	$2.99	☐
HP#11632	THE SHINING OF LOVE by Emma Darcy	$2.99	☐
HR#03265	HERO ON THE LOOSE by Rebecca Winters	$2.89	☐
HR#03268	THE BAD PENNY by Susan Fox	$2.99	☐
HS#70532	TOUCH THE DAWN by Karen Young	$3.39	☐
HS#70576	ANGELS IN THE LIGHT by Margot Dalton	$3.50	☐
HI#22249	MUSIC OF THE MIST by Laura Pender	$2.99	☐
HI#22267	CUTTING EDGE by Caroline Burnes	$2.99	☐
HAR#16489	DADDY'S LITTLE DIVIDEND by Elda Minger	$3.50	☐
HAR#16525	CINDERMAN by Anne Stuart	$3.50	☐
HH#28801	PROVIDENCE by Miranda Jarrett	$3.99	☐
HH#28775	A WARRIOR'S QUEST by Margaret Moore	$3.99	☐

(limited quantities available on certain titles)

TOTAL AMOUNT	$
DEDUCT: 10% DISCOUNT FOR 2+ BOOKS	$
POSTAGE & HANDLING	$
($1.00 for one book, 50¢ for each additional)	
APPLICABLE TAXES*	$_____
TOTAL PAYABLE	$_____

(check or money order—please do not send cash)

To order, complete this form and send it, along with a check or money order for the total above, payable to Harlequin Books, to: **In the U.S.:** 3010 Walden Avenue, P.O. Box 9047, Buffalo, NY 14269-9047; **In Canada:** P.O. Box 613, Fort Erie, Ontario, L2A 5X3.

Name: _____

Address:_____City: _____

State/Prov.: _____ Zip/Postal Code: _____

*New York residents remit applicable sales taxes.
 Canadian residents remit applicable GST and provincial taxes.

"*Mr. Blake—*"

"Mr. Blake?" His blond eyebrows raked sardonically upward. "Why so formal all of a sudden? What happened to 'you big oaf' and 'Neanderthal'...darling?"

The snarled endearment was definitely a threat.

"I—I suppose you've spoken to that detective—"

"We had a fascinating conversation. Now where are they?"

"W-who?"

"Not who, what! And don't bother running that doe-eyed-innocence routine past me. I don't buy it. If you don't start cooperating I'll have you thrown behind bars so fast, your head will spin!"

No need—it was spinning wildly already. Doe-eyed? No one had ever called her that before. If it hadn't been yelled with such insulting emphasis, she might have mistaken it for a compliment.

SUSAN NAPIER was born on St. Valentine's Day, so it's not surprising she has developed an enduring love of romantic stories. She started her writing career as a journalist in Auckland, New Zealand, trying her hand at romance fiction only after she had married her handsome boss! Numerous books later she still lives with her most enduring hero, two future heroes—her sons!—two cats and a computer. When she's not writing, she likes to read and cook, often simultaneously!

Books by Susan Napier

Don't miss any of our special offers. Write to us at the following address for information on our newest releases.

Harlequin Reader Service
U.S.: 3010 Walden Ave., P.O. Box 1325, Buffalo, NY 14269
Canadian: P.O. Box 609, Fort Erie, Ont. L2A 5X3